S0-DUJ-148

Suburban Death

tkins, Meg Elizabeth.
Suburban death /

005. WITHDRAWN
3305212061091
i   02/14/07

Suburban Death

MEG ELIZABETH ATKINS

First published in Great Britain in 2005 by
Allison & Busby Limited
Bon Marché Centre
241-251 Ferndale Road
London SW9 8BJ
http://www.allisonandbusby.com

Copyright © 2005 by MEG ELIZABETH ATKINS

The moral right of the author has been asserted.

This book is sold subject to the conditions that it shall not,
by way of trade or otherwise, be lent, resold, hired out or
otherwise circulated without the publisher's prior
written consent in any form of binding or cover other than
that in which it is published and without a similar condition
being imposed upon the subsequent
purchaser.

A catalogue record for this book is available from
the British Library.

10 9 8 7 6 5 4 3 2 1

ISBN 0 7490 8207 0

Printed and bound in Wales by
Creative Print and Design, Ebbw Vale

MEG ELIZABETH ATKINS is a full-time writer who currently lives in Lincolnshire. The author of many acclaimed novels, *Suburban Death* is the latest in the crime series featuring DCI Sheldon Hunter and his team.

Also by Meg Elisabeth Atkins

Private View

The dedication that went missing has at
last found its way home here:

With love to my friend

Mags Watson

In the somnolent afternoon the tree-lined, curving, quiet streets of Bankhill were utopian terrain for pelting bicycles.

People were resting, or reading, or having tea; in the abundant gardens they were drifting to and fro in hammocks, or sunbathing on velvet lawns. Their world, hushed and private, dreamed behind ranges of laurel and syringa, scented by rose and honeysuckle.

With panting, violent striving the two boys, big for eleven, well dressed, had raced each other round the Quadrant – its shops shuttered by Wednesday early closing – past the lido and the Roxy Cinema and were heading for the golf links, where the houses were older, stood farther apart and between their top-heavy old trees gave glimpses of the distant wooded rise of Alderley Edge.

They called each other Stinky and Carp. Stinky because he was always farting – what boy didn't – but even among his contemporaries he was an epic performer. Carp – this was a new word, a get-one-over-on-adults hugely enjoyable crudity because Carp was a mangled version of Crap, which they were not allowed to say.

There was a lexicon of words that were supposed not to exist but had entered eager young minds by devious channels; everyone knew them, had an approximate understanding of their meanings. Prohibitions and commands were the province of controlling adults: parents, teachers, clergymen, doctors. The subservient adults – workmen, tradesmen, cleaners, shop keepers, used the words cheerfully with sly, knowing looks that hinted at a world of lurid experiences and rude explanations.

Their birthdays were close together. Carp was riding his present, a shining Raleigh with a Sturmey Archer three speed, cable brakes and hub dynamo. Stinky's present was a 35mm Kodak camera, long yearned for, at last achieved by means which he had no trouble blanking from his consciousness.

And then, rounding the bend of Bloomsbury Avenue, they

came upon the rapidly closing rear view of a plump, comfortable lady, cycling sedately...

There was a game played deplorably through that hot, endless summer by boys on bicycles, never by girls. The boys sped, noiseless but for the hissing of tyres, caught up with the cyclist ahead – then swooped close, elbowing, yelling terrifyingly. The object of the game was the glee of seeing the victim tilt, crash to the ground... Male or female, it didn't matter, the imperative adult world was momentarily reduced to thrashing legs, wrenching gasps, a glimpse of sensible knickers, flying spectacles, rucked clothing, capsized dignity.

For Stinky and Carp it was their first strike. They had always, after whispered dares, lost their nerve, made excuses, urged...

And now it was Stinky who, adrenaline charged, darted into the lead, snatching Carp in his wake on the unspoken, urgent *now, now* —

And it was Stinky, in the hurtling immediacy of the aftermath, who turned on a lightning reflex, lifted his Kodak to commemorate her.

She was lying half on the road, her head on the pavement edge decorated with a breath-taking splurge of blood.

Carp braked, wobbling. A wrenched backward glance. 'But – she's – hurt —'

Stinky said with low-voiced triumph, 'You can't hurt that old cow, she's always falling over, she just gets up again and —'

While he was speaking Carp was skittering backwards on his Raleigh, stopping, looking down. 'Stinky, she's *bleeding*.'

And there it began, that golden afternoon, on a headlong impulse – but who was to say without some hidden, malign intent – that set the route to the destruction of inoffensive lives.

Chapter Two

'Darlings,' Floy Mannering's sweet voice, 'You do this so beautifully.'

'This' was not just the tea – china set out exquisitely on a handmade lace cloth; cucumber sandwiches and smoked salmon rolls, scones and cream and strawberries – it was Daisy herself, in her caressing afternoon frock, unhurried, wryly amused. And Clive, in his blazer and crisp flannels. Floy had a way of suggesting that Daisy was responsible for him, but she was not; he had presented himself, as Daisy had, out of love for Floy, her generosity and kindness, her care for their feelings. And Floy...the passing years defined her narrow elegance, added repose to her delicate face and a fugitive youthfulness to her smile.

Floy's friends, the Prendergasts, were coming on one of their ceremonial visits. Tea and gossip. Whist. More gossip. And then, 'A sherry to see you on your way?'

In Floy's stylish house, friends and neighbours slipped sympathetically into place – if they were eccentric period pieces there were so many of them they went unnoticed. Clive once said to Daisy, 'Do you think they're all steadily getting more bonkers? Or are we just imagining it?'

'The whole of Bankhill is bonkers – well, the older residents – they accept almost anything.'

The afternoon visit over, the Prendergasts ushered gently on their straight-backed retreat, Daisy went into the dining room to clear the remains of the tea, looked out of the window at the figure marching round the curve of the drive, round the tall conifers that shielded the road from view. She moaned, 'Oh, no,' and dashed into the hall.

She found Clive, seized him for a frantically muted consultation.

He said, 'Can't we get rid of her?'

'How? She just barges in the minute the door's opened.'

'Could I interpose my body?'

'Not if you value your jangly bits. She'd knee you soon as look at you. Do you honestly want – have you ever taken on Grendel's mother?'

'Darlings, what is it?' Floy emerged from the downstairs cloakroom.

Daisy paused, caught out, said helplessly, 'Um…Edward's Auntie Brenda.'

'Ah.' For a moment Floy looked cornered, then resigned. 'It really is naughty of you to call her after a monster in a Norse epic. Beowulf, isn't it? Although you happen to be right.'

The doorbell shrilled. The three stood quite still, looking at one another. Floy said philosophically, 'Oh well, perhaps you'll have a brainwave how to get rid of her. Don't hesitate, will you?'

She turned away to the lounge hall on the – to Daisy – glorious assumption that the momentum of the dependable everyday would carry matters forward, that either Daisy or Clive would open the door, murmur obligatory greetings, show the visitor in.

Daisy's mother, now living in Portugal, was Floy's best friend, although she was many years younger. Daisy had had a lifetime of testing the fine filaments of which Floy Mannering was made – knew the elegance and gentleness, how a situation within hailing distance of havoc could be contained, subdued: *let them eat cake*. That was just about it, that was what happened, between one ring of the doorbell and the next. Floy limped across the hall, Clive disappeared upstairs, and Daisy coped, opened the door.

'I see you've had comp'ny. I passed those two old fossils in the drive.'

Brenda Hutton, née Skinner, said, thrusting forward. A small, battling, bosomy woman with hard features and immovably sculptured hairdo, she worked at a hairdressers called Twirlies off the main Chatfield road where the spreading Easton estate met the new by-pass. She was not speaking to Daisy, who was the only person in sight, she was simply establishing her presence vocally. Shoving Daisy aside with a glance of dismissive dislike she tilted herself forwards on the wobble of dangerously high heels, surged across the parquet-floored entrance hall, past the gate-legged table with its china bowl of roses and the tall, sinuous Art Nouveau jardinière and sweeping fern.

Beyond the archway to one side of the open well staircase stood the lounge hall, oak panelled, beamed ceiling, old brick fireplace. A friend, a valued neighbour, would have been entertained there, or in the informality of the garden room, at ease in cushioned wicker chairs, admiring the private, dreaming garden through the long French windows.

But this was the charade of an afternoon visit. Daisy, as a good head taller physically in command, diverted Brenda to the study at the other side of the hall. Not an inch of Fairmead lacked elegance; the study was a purposeful ordering of bookshelves and serious leather armchairs, few ornaments, no vases of flowers, the delicate satinwood secretaire Floy's mother had chosen for herself.

The first time Daisy had shown Brenda into there she had noted her face set in pugilistic rejection as she flinched from the rows of books, with: 'What's the good of that lot?'

'I think they'd be for reading, don't you?' she said, her brilliant smile lost on Brenda who was glaring everywhere except at her. The seed of mischief was planted; afterwards, Daisy always took her into the study.

Brenda made a rasping sound, muttered something about no use nor bloody ornament, tried to peer round Daisy to catch a glimpse of the hall. 'I came to see the organ-grinder, not the monkey.'

'I'll tell her that, she'll find it so amusing,' Daisy said sweetly, leaving the room at once with the pleasurable thought of Brenda sitting alone in swivel-eyed uneasiness, convinced the books were capable of sneaking up and grappling her to the ground. With the air of getting the unavoidable over as quickly as possible, Floy was crossing the hall. Daisy said under her breath, 'Tea?' Floy pulled a monster face.

Volubly mendacious, Brenda ignored Daisy and concerned herself with Floy's hip operation. 'How *are* you? You're doing so well,' and then, after wearying nothings, launched upon her unswervable purpose. Her nephew Edward. 'Our Ed's likely to come for a visit, he's in London on business.'

Ed's business was something Floy never concerned herself with, not because it was beyond her interest or understanding, but because, in ways she preferred to leave uncomprehended, it involved her dear cousin Aquilla.

'And I know you always like news of him, as he's your sister Reenie's adopted son, so to speak. Her marrying too late to have her own.' It was something she always made sure to say, with a small, triumphant smile.

And Floy answered, as always, from her collected good manners, 'No, as you must remember. Irene —' the subtle emphasis on the name, reclaiming it to the family pronunciation: I-reen, 'never adopted Edward. By marrying his father, she became his stepmother.'

'Oh, well.' A sharp gesture. 'Same thing. Family anyway. Makes us related, doesn't it?' She always made sure of saying that, too, in one form or another. She glanced extravagantly at her winking diamanté watch. 'Our John'll be picking me up shortly —'

Daisy registered – not for the first time – how Brenda made arrangements regardless of anything Floy had to do. The phone rang distantly, at once silenced: Clive must have picked up the extension. Daisy yearned for escape but would not, if she could help it, leave Floy.

The Mannering and Skinner family convolutions were beyond her, she had been at the receiving end of them since childhood visits with her mother. In those days, helplessly aware of nothing except her hindrance to her mother's acting career – the supreme misnomer for an erratic course that, too often, threatened homelessness, had it not been for Floy.

But over those years of dumped 'visits' and 'holidays', at first not even sure who Ed was, she had absorbed a notion of headlong, unstoppable force – from where? His family: strident people who called Floy 'Aunt Florrie,' which Floy loathed, had bad manners and didn't like anyone except themselves.

As a child she found herself so often in the role of comforter to Floy, although, in the swirling crosscurrents she could do nothing except sit quietly holding Floy's hand. She resolved that when she grew up, she would act as Floy's protector, stop these awful people invading Fairmead. In fact, there were not many, it was only on an appalled reflex she imagined they spread everywhere, and stuck, like porridge.

In reality there were: Brenda; her husband Arthur; and her two children, John and – Sheila? – plonked down to crawl and brawl, grow from raging toddlers to grunting adolescents. Then the perpetual, excruciating family events: Christmas; wedding; anniversary; from which, as far as Daisy knew, Floy managed to be absent. Unwell, holiday… And if Daisy was staying, and it was *totally unavoidable* – something solemn, a funeral – she went, too, buttressing Floy, speechlessly admiring her dignity.

And through all the years, in and out of these occasions, the swooping visit, vivid as a kingfisher, of glamorous, blond Edward.

Brenda leaned forward comfortingly to Floy, 'Well, I asked our John to come for me. I know you couldn't take me home as you're in no state to drive.'

'Oh – um – Daisy – would —' Floy's light, melodious voice was ideally tuned for helpful but incomplete utterances.

Brenda spared Daisy a contemptuous look. 'Drive, do you? I thought you just —' She waved a bracelet clattered wrist.

'Did the housework?' Daisy suggested brightly.

'Well, you're not family. Not related, are you?'

The door opened, minimally, Clive's voice floated cheerfully, 'Floy, sorry to interrupt. Phone call.'

Daisy slipped out, swiftly overtaking his retreat towards the stairs. 'It isn't one of Brenda's ghastly progeny looking for her, is it? Tell them they can have her.'

'Course not, Dado, I'd tell her myself —'

No, you wouldn't. But you wouldn't dump them on Floy.

'— it's Quill. You don't need to remind Floy, leave him on hold too long and leprechauns eat the telephone line. I've had a good chat with him.'

It took Floy time to get out of her chair, then she paused, cast about, not sure if this was a ruse. Sometimes, the effort of dislodging Brenda made her subject to surreal fantasies: the house could be on fire, plague break out in Bankhill with consequent mass evacuation…

To her parents, loved, long dead, she had been the ideal, obedient daughter, lavished and protected. But her bold sister Irene, determined on a teaching career, independence, had, in achieving her ambition, disrupted the family equilibrium. That was long ago, but its consequence persisted to the present, trapping Floy in the company of this offensive woman.

Daisy, reading Floy's perplexed face, saw she would have to be practical – a motivation sometimes beautifully mislaid at Fairmead. 'Floy, it's Aquilla.'

Floy's immediate, delighted smile... Her cousin, Sir Aquilla Mannering, resident in Ireland, too seldom seen.

'Clive's been talking to him. Now you go and have a good gossip.'

'Yes, yes,' Floy said, and to Brenda, 'please excuse me.'

Before going into the kitchen, Daisy shut Brenda into the study to do whatever impelled her. Flick through a magazine. Stare through the diamond paned windows at the screen of conifers. More likely sit fuming. Another thought – Daisy gave in to the impulse to test it – and slipped from the kitchen.

The study door was now open a few inches. Brenda's diamanté earring glittered where she stood straining towards the sound of Floy's voice across the hall.

Unlike Brenda, Daisy had the advantage of every dearly loved inch of Fairmead, could soft-foot her way through its geography, spring upon any eavesdropper. A new distress, overturning years of unquestioning trust: *why should anyone want to eavesdrop?*

She flung open the door. 'Oh, gosh, sorry, Brenda. Didn't think you'd be there.'

Brenda staggered back on her insecure heels, glared, then adopted an air of inappropriate coyness. 'Er – the toilet?'

'Heavens, of course.' Daisy grabbed, guided her breakneck through the hall, past the telephone alcove, talking loudly. 'I'll wait outside – the catch is a bit wobbly – people always getting locked in. Banging on the door for hours if we're somewhere else in the house. Or in the garden. No, I insist, not at all —' Registering Floy, speaking on the phone, uncharacteristically raising her voice, baffled either by Daisy's invention about the catch on the lavatory door or Aquilla's frequently eccentric telephone connection.

Emerging from the cloakroom Brenda, venting her feelings, snapped, 'This house is like a mausoleum.'

'Don't you mean museum?' Daisy asked carefully.

'All the bloody same.' She would never have said this to Floy, to whom her attitude was cautious, sycophantic – and – Daisy for no reason sometimes felt – untraceably threatening.

Chapter Three

Depositing Brenda back in the study and closing the door on her with deliberation, Daisy went into the kitchen and found Brenda's son John there. He never came to the front door but always walked round the side and let himself in without bothering to knock. The kitchen door stood open, anyway, to pick up whatever vagrant breeze carried the scent of roses from the garden.

John, a short young man with jowls and a beer belly, spectacles on an expressionless face, asked, 'Me mam here?' directing the question somewhere in Daisy's vicinity. Like his mother he managed seldom to actually look at her.

Daisy circled round until she was standing directly in front of him, stared fixedly at his averted face. 'Yes.'

He grunted, sat down at the kitchen table, helping himself to anything within reach, chomping through the left-overs Daisy had not yet put away. He never had anything to say to her; she once pointed out to Clive that he had the conversational skills of a garden gnome. His pale, bulging eyes roamed, searching for shortcomings. He usually found something. She waited.

'Why yer 'ave that on in summer?'

'It's an Aga. We cook in it. Like, um, an oven,' she said carefully.

Silence. He chewed, swallowed, gaze fixed on the Aga.

'We turn our oven off when we're not cookin'.'

Argument? Explanation? Query? She gave up, sorted crockery, cutlery, put dishes and silver away. Shortly, impelled by her maternal instinct, Brenda walked in. 'Thought you'd be making yourself at home,' she said complacently to her son. 'How's your Shirley? Is her cough better?' She had huge pride in her immediate family, interlocked by tribal allegiance and shrieking fights.

They talked, congratulated each other on the cleverness of his children, the perfection of his home, his wife Enid's housekeeping excellence. Ignored, helplessly exposed to doings that were no concern of hers, Daisy put the kitchen to rights, thought of Clive, secreting himself upstairs.

Oh, why doesn't he come down, with his wit, his charm?

Why is he hiding?

Shall I kill myself now?

The verbal miasma (it wasn't a conversation – was it?) had taken on a stridency that forced itself on her attention. Something to do with a neighbour of the Skinners who was in trouble with the police. Brenda said, forcefully, 'Don't have nothing to do with the filth. If they're about, anywhere, you keep right away. And say nothing. Nothing. Right?'

John nodded, a clockwork response. 'Yeh.'

Daisy took some puzzled account of this while they reverted to the intricacies of their domestic affairs; then she switched off, crushingly bored.

Floy came in, greeted John with surprised politeness, 'I didn't realise you were here —' her voice drowned by Brenda's cloying concern, 'And how's Quillie?'

'Oh, yes, Quill's very well. Yes, rather, he's – er —' Floy wilted beneath Brenda's gimlet gaze. John, staring at Floy, continued eating anything within reach. Floy said, 'Unfortunately, we were cut off, we had so little time, I've never understood why his telephone is so unreliable —'

'Floy, sit down,' Daisy said firmly.

Floy sat, said, 'Yes, but Quill's awfully well.' And tumbling words in her pleasure – he could be coming for a visit, it had been such a long time since they'd seen him. Of course, they were always in touch, letters, mostly yes, and phone calls, but – nothing was quite like seeing him…

Brenda's voice rapped, 'Our Edward didn't say he was coming here. Are you sure? Quillie can't be doing something without Edward knowing.'

Daisy stared. Floy began a stammered explanation, 'Well, you see, I had so few words with Aquilla himself before – you see, the phone – and then we were cut off…'

Daisy shouted silently, *Floy, don't explain yourself to this awful person.*

Brenda snapped at John, 'Did our Edward say anything to you

about Quillie coming here? When he rang on Wednesday and I was out. Did he?'

John, his mouth full of currant bread, shook his head.

'There, you see, Flo, he'd tell his own nephew, wouldn't he? Ed would tell his own nephew. You got it wrong.'

Aching to spring to Floy's defence, infuriatingly helpless, Daisy swallowed the words: *What's it got to do with Edward?* Because as far as she and Floy understood, with tentative assent but minimum discussion, was that Quill and Edward had ended their association. But she could scarcely start an argument on such a personal matter, it would be like inviting the objectionable Skinner mother and son into their personal lives.

Brenda persisted, addressing Floy in an offensively loud voice, 'You've got it wrong, love.'

Daisy said clearly, 'Floy has had a hip operation, not a lobotomy.'

'What's that?' John asked his mother.

'Take no notice. That'll be it, Flo, with the line being bad and everything, easy to get things mixed up.'

'Oh, no,' Floy said, gently persistent. 'You see, I've spoken to Clive, who had a good chat with him first…and what he had managed to sort out was that Aquilla wasn't definitely coming over, but might because he was worrying about the deteriorating health of his old friend, Hugh Stephenson.'

'Hugh Stephenson, him,' Brenda sniffed. Her face suddenly sharp, 'He's in that nursing home, the Manor, isn't he? Ga-ga, I daresay by now.'

'He's had a stroke, well, he had one a year ago, and he was recovering so splendidly, then he recently had a second one —'

'That's what I said, ga-ga. Why doesn't Quillie just phone him, instead of coming all this way?' Brenda suggested with strenuous good sense.

If she had met Hugh Stephenson, Daisy could not recall it, but she was honour bound to defend anyone in the Mannering web of friends and relations. She said coldly to John, 'A stroke patient can suffer from dysphasia. That means,' she continued, as he stared somewhere beyond her shoulder, his mouth open, 'he might find it difficult to articulate.'

'What's that?'

'Speak.'

'Like old Mr Jones,' John said to his mother. 'He just makes noises like eergh – nnyaah – yeesh.'

'Who does?' Floy asked, staring at him with the look of a woman struggling out of a nightmare.

'Old Mr Jones,' John muttered to the table.

'Well, there you are then,' Brenda said, as if something irksome had been packed away.

Being sensible, as the only possible alternative to emptying a jug over Brenda, Daisy suggested to Floy, 'Would you like to go and see Hugh? Then you can tell Quill —'

Leaning towards Floy, tapping her arm in a rude semaphore, Brenda said, 'Don't you go running errands, not in your state. 'Sides, how would you get there? Oh, I forgot —' she leaned towards John, her voice cloying, 'She drives, Miss Thingummy here —'

'Donovan. The name's Donovan,' Daisy said clearly.

Brenda ignored her, 'Isn't she the clever one? Drives.'

'Enid wouldn't do nothing like that,' John said stolidly.

'No, course not. But she doesn't just...' Brenda cast a look around the kitchen, then smiled pityingly, nodding in Daisy's direction: the poor relation battening on a generous relative. Daisy's anger instantly reduced to a yell of laughter she had to turn into a fit of coughing.

By the time she recovered, Brenda was again tapping Floy's arm, 'He never was up to much, that Hugh Stephenson, you couldn't trust anything he said, all smarmy. Oh, I know he was a *posh* photographer, but how long ago was that? He's nothing now, you don't want to be bothered with him.'

Floy attempted to remove her arm, but Brenda now clutched it, crumpling the silk of Floy's dress.

Too quickly to meet with resistance, Daisy went to Floy's side, took Brenda's wrist and detached her hand, 'Floy, you're tired, it's time you had a rest.'

Taken by surprise, Brenda glared, speechless; even something approaching expression crossed John's face.

Daisy said brisk things about I know you'll excuse Floy and you'll see yourselves out, making sure they did. Usually they left with blustering energy and raucous laughter, satisfied by having stamped their presence on Fairmead; this time there was a sullenness, and before the door closed Brenda's carrying voice, 'Who does she think she is, pushing me about, near enough assault that was —'

Floy was limping into the hall, her face strained.

Aware that the last thing she wanted was anger and carping, Daisy said gently, 'You always have so much fun when the Prendergasts visit. And then, these – Skinners – they – just sabotage – everything.'

'It's all right, darling. I'm tired, that's all. I need to lie down.'

Having enough sense to know when she couldn't mend matters, Daisy helped Floy to her room, drew curtains, went to the games room in search of Clive.

Chapter Four

In the games room at Fairmead the permanent collided with the transitional, retaining traces of all who had passed through it. How many? Uncounted relatives. Then to Daisy's knowledge: Clive. Aquilla. Daisy's mother during her many emotional shipwrecks. Fairmead was haven and Floy generous with hospitality. My dear, there's no hurry. Do stay…

But Clive, his journey through boyhood to independence, always so close to Floy; unsettled, needing somewhere to house his belongings, insensibly claimed the games room as his own territory – simply because there was more of his stuff there than anyone else's, invading shelves, cupboards…His John Bull printing set, his Hornby trains, his Dinky toy collection, his Meccano. Books: Haggard, Henty, Bulldog Drummond, Buchan – the cherished inheritance of uncles, grandparents. Comics: the *Magnet*, *Gem*, *Hotspur*. Bound editions of the *Boy's Own Paper* so luggingly weighty no one had disturbed the pile for years.

(Daisy had once been delighted to discover amongst such innocent diversions a banned first edition of *Lady Chatterly's Lover*. She wondered who it could possibly have belonged to.)

And amongst this tide of artefacts and commemoration – not specific to Clive – a dismantled ping pong table; a folding cane and bamboo screen, a dappled rocking horse with lost tail, a Jones treadle sewing machine, a Bakelite wireless, a cabin trunk crammed with magazines: *Woman's Weekly*, *Men Only*, *Picture Post*, *Lilliput*…

It was there, in the accumulation of memory, that Daisy was assailed by the vulnerability of Floy's life, the long past now obscurely menaced by the Skinners and their thuggish insistence on family ties. Undetailed stories carried their own freight of meaning: Floy's childhood, cosseted, protected, her inherited affluence, enviable, yes – but the gaze of a later generation gave back the picture of an unfulfilled woman.

Daisy's account to Clive of what had occurred with Brenda and John, accompanied by striding and swearing, gradually lost its frantic edge. This was no place for it, why should the Skinners trespass here: the breathing quiet, the windows full of sunlight and dust motes, the corners full of vanished incidents, Clive's murmured sympathy.

He went to the tall wooden cupboard, decorated with fading pictures of characters and scenes from *Alice* and *Wind in the Willows*. It had once held Floy and Irene's toys, long passed to the less fortunate, sold in charitable jumble sales, thrown away – one or two hoarded, cherished in Floy's room. An accumulation of stray objects had been pushed into it; Clive opened the one cupboard he kept for his own use, produced a bottle of claret and glasses, said, 'You've earned this. Stout fella, services beyond the call of duty. Dado, darling, families are hell.'

'Some, yes, but not ours.'

'Ours' was not even hers, but Daisy needed the anchor of her mother's friendship with Floy, to be valued by the Mannerings, to give her love and loyalty to them.

'And they're not family, only the most distant – just Irene marrying – well – and that was a million years ago —'

'Thirty-one,' Clive murmured.

'Well, that's not enough to constitute a bloody life sentence for Floy. So. Aquilla wants to visit Hugh – why shouldn't he? They've been friends since, since, before the Flood, for God's sake. Well, you remember when you and Edward were boys how close they were. And how long since they've seen each other?'

'Oh, I don't know Daisy. Years. You know how Quill prefers to stay tucked away in Ireland. His beloved hunting.'

She could refute this from personal knowledge. 'Quill's been too frail to ride for ages. It must be important, mustn't it? That he wants to see Hugh. And Floy's trying to do her best, but she's still not strong and...' running out of patience, she hissed, 'What is it about those Skinners? Why do they come across as such effing vampires?'

Clive shrugged, resigned. 'Daisy, you couldn't be more right.'

'Hey – she thinks I'm the hired help. I should be in a wrap-around pinnie and turban.'

He said with concern, 'She can't – I mean – what does she think Mrs Lowe does here three mornings a week? And surely she must know you're going to open your dancing school in Chatfield this autumn.'

'How? Floy wouldn't tell her. Anything. Neither would I. Would you?'

'God, no. But you can't let her put you down.'

Clive was lovingly supportive of her enterprise, advising her, sharing her plans with her business partner, Ellie Clarke, (they had trained at the Dance Academy together) who was working out a contract in San Francisco. He offered to lend her money, which she declined, with the proviso that if she got stuck, she'd ask. She went regularly to the run-down dancing school she and Ellie were taking over – to keep her feet in, Clive said – and often he went with her.

'Her opinion means damn all to me. Does it mean a gnat's fart to you? No. Quite. I'm not going to explain myself to her. I don't think she'd believe anything I said, anyway.'

He agreed, picked up an untidy wodge of papers, albums, large envelopes. 'Must run, love. Date.' His free arm encircled her in a bear hug, he was tall, elegantly well-built; for Daisy there had always been comfort and pleasure in being close to him.

She hugged back and they grappled, giggling. Daisy said, 'La, sir. Cease. I shall be forced to strike you with my reticule.'

'Don't you know you can drive a man mad, you minx.'

'I suppose your date's that lovely young man who's just joined the tennis club.'

'Yup.'

'Oh, well,' boyfriendless, Daisy said glumly: 'Lucky old you. I fancied him but he just didn't know I was there. Who does.'

'Hey, Dado. You're lovely, you could have anyone.'

'Really? The only ones I know about are ghastly —' she swooped to rescue papers slipping from his grasp. 'Is all this stuff the Bankhill recollections you were talking about?'

'Might just be something useful. Could all be rubbish. I'm not sure I'm altogether sold on the project.'

'Mmm. Because it comes into your definition of hand-knitted. But you know how people love it. All those sweet little books you've done, people writing about their great aunt Mrs Alderman

Blatby Grind – and the photos – *Postwomen in World War One. Uncle Jim and his grocery van, with Nutty the horse.* Enchanting. And they all sold out.'

Years before, Clive gave up an unhappy career in the Civil Service, moved back from London to Chatfield and took over a publishing firm from a near moribund Mannering relative. With a partner, strictly business, he began to liven up the worthy, static publications: *Strolls around Knutsford. An Edwardian childhood in Great Budworth. Trace your Ancestors* – this, Clive maintained, pandering to someone's inexplicable need to prove kinship with a stay-maker in Nantwich. Why should he encourage them?

He had the judgement to retain the traditional links: footpaths through timeless landscapes, dreaming idylls, grand estates. He developed a speciality sideline, arranging motoring parties for lunch or tea at country homes of personal connections. Sweetly and shamelessly he plundered present and past, friend and stranger; everyone loved him, trusted him. Except, of course, the Skinners. Daisy had once ferociously absorbed the knowledge, without conscious acquisition, that they referred to him as 'that queer nancy boy'.

They kissed goodbye and, alone, Daisy poured herself another glass of wine and considered, baffled.

They both adored Floy – and yet Clive always found excuses not to be involved with the Skinners, not even to see them if he could avoid it. As an outsider she was not entitled to make judgements, but – as an outsider – she could take an uncommitted view.

Sometimes she suspected it was something to do with Floy as principal beneficiary of the Mannering will. But of course, no one would be so vulgar as to talk money with Floy.

What Daisy did know, culled from various sources, was that the Mannering parents, distrustful of Irene's boldness and independence, left their considerable property and money in trust to both Floy and Irene. Then, when she was supposed to have settled into unassailable spinsterhood, Irene quietly took herself off to the Register Office and married Stanley Crane, whose wife, a Skinner, had died two years previously. A sweet

man, but amongst the Mannerings, to a susurration of concern –
a carpenter, not someone with a profession. Furthermore,
through no fault of his own, he was not commercially minded;
the long strain of his first wife's illness, her death, of trying to care
for his young son Edward, became too much for him, his
business suffered, he was declared bankrupt.

Nevertheless, Irene went ahead with the marriage, she was
determined and strong-willed, more than capable of bringing
order to dishevelled lives. The short marriage, to everyone's
surprise, was radiantly fulfilled. The reticent Mannerings added
up the value of this and were always happy on Irene's behalf.

Then Irene's shockingly accidental death was a blow too hard
for Stanley to bear, he survived her by only seven months, which
left Edward an orphan.

From her mother's occasional confidences, family gossip,
hushed asides, Daisy absorbed the idea that the Skinners had
assumed Edward would be adequately provided for by Irene.
Perhaps he had been. But no one seemed to be responsible for
him, as far as she understood he had been fielded out to various
Skinners, circulating in ways unknown to Daisy, who had no
contact and no interest.

Another assumption had been that as Clive and Edward were
such friends, and Irene was Floy's sister, Floy would make a home
for Edward. But that had not happened and no one, in Daisy's
hearing, had ever spoken of it. Years later, when she was in her
twenties and staying at Fairmead, Floy took her out to supper at
her favourite restaurant. It had been Irene's, too, and it was
natural they should talk of Irene and then, somehow, it became
the right time to speak, briefly, of Edward.

He had not been, Floy confided, a nice boy. Charming, yes, he
inherited that from his father – with Stanley it was genuine, with
Edward it was, well… That was the clever thing, it seemed
genuine, but in reality, so very calculated.

'Irene was always kind to him, scrupulously fair, but – she was
accustomed to being treated with respect, and I'm afraid
Edward… Of course, he had been made a great deal of by his
family after Vera – his mother's – death, which I think is only

right. His grandparents were the exception. Awfully forbidding, they seemed to resent Stanley because he was ten years older than their daughter, and a steadier, kinder man you couldn't…'

Daisy refilled Floy's glass. 'You didn't know them then, when Edward's mother died, did you?'

'Oh, no, I never met any of them until Irene married Stanley. The grandparents gave no comfort to either Stanley or Edward after Vera's death. I learnt this later, from other sources, and quite candidly, Daisy, I wasn't in the least bit interested, but it did seem to me so unfeeling, They seemed to have a bottomless well of disapproval because they transferred it to Irene. She was strong, you know, she could cope with anyone. It amused her they considered her posh beyond words, Stanley a traitor to his class. Although I don't think they'd quite have put it like that. They'd always been so critical of Edward, they were worse when Irene married his father, started referring to him as "spoilt namby pamby," putting on airs. Then after his father's death, they had a belated change of heart, he was suddenly a poor motherless lad, needing their protection and indulgence. Thank you, darling, just a smidgeon,' as Daisy topped up her glass. 'Pity you have to drive, we should have thought to take a taxi. I was glad for his sake, but I must say, nobody much seemed to want him when he was orphaned. And I'll be completely candid, I couldn't contemplate – a schoolboy – if it had been a girl, someone like you, not that there is, but they…'

As Daisy was about to ask all kinds of questions about why the grandparents had not taken the motherless lad under their own roof but left him to be shuffled around amongst the rest of the family, two friends of Floy's appeared – do let's have coffee together. And the moment passed.

Chapter Five

After Brenda's visit, Floy said nothing about visiting Hugh; Daisy took tactful account of this. On the third morning she picked up the *Daily Telegraph* and post to put on Floy's breakfast tray. She never sorted through the post, it seemed sneaky, intrusive, when all of it was for Floy. If there was a letter from Ellie, the occasional letter or card from friends or – rarely – her mother, Floy was only too pleased to hand it to her, 'Something for you, darling, how nice.'

She carried the tray into Floy, drew back the curtains to a golden morning. They had a gossip, talked of their arrangements, Daisy would shop, later drive Floy to her poetry reading group. Then she asked tentatively, 'Have you thought any more about going to see Hugh?'

'No, well…I will see…soon…perhaps…'

Daisy nodded and changed the subject; Fairmead seduced time, everything that happened there happened in its own sequence, which might, or might not conform with reality.

After making arrangements for the day, Daisy left her to herself.

The habit of reticence did not allow her to draw attention to a cheap, ill-typed envelope – Floy supported so many charities. When, after an hour there was no sign of her, Daisy returned to find her still in bed.

She seemed suddenly to rouse, snatching at the *Telegraph* in pretence of reading it, a crumpled envelope fumbled away into the sheets. She had eaten scarcely anything, her cup of coffee stood cold on the bedside table. Her face was pale as ivory.

'Floy, what is it? You look —'

'I'm just, not quite feeling…'

'Shall I phone Doctor Evans —'

'Goodness, no, don't fuss, there's a dear. I need to be quiet for a while.'

'Yes, yes. You do whatever…'

Daisy took the tray to the kitchen, tried abstractedly to write out a shopping list; after a while gave up and made herself coffee.

She was rather afraid of her own helplessness in the face of Floy's unaccountable change: the good spirits of the morning, the chat, the plans – and now that pleasant prospect of the day suddenly undone.

Perhaps it was the association, here in the kitchen…

A surge of rage. Yes, she was chronically inclined to attribute *anything* unpleasant to the Skinners, but the fact remained that the last time Floy had worn that cornered look had been when Brenda and John marauded Fairmead with their unpleasantness and rudeness. After relieving her feelings to Clive, Daisy had dismissed the episode, not spoken of it to Floy, who would scarcely want to be reminded. Inexplicable as it was, it had occurred and was over and done with.

But, as a way of constructively calming herself, Daisy put together its elements.

Brenda's outrage that Edward didn't know Quill was intending to visit Hugh Stephenson.

Her denigration of Hugh – *ga-ga, you can't trust anything he says* – what a cruel and unfeeling way to speak to Floy of an old friend.

And why, for heaven's sake, should she be so determined to prevent Floy visiting Hugh? What business was it of hers?

Floy had been brought up in the tradition of dignified civility that made confidences impossible. Her inner self was private territory; her social contacts informed by charm and good manners, always a sympathetic ear for other people's troubles. The hidden Floy, amongst her contemporaries, might be a searing, stripped-down gossip, but the idea was so outlandish it made Daisy laugh, feebly.

Short of saying: Look here Floy, what is all this about you and the Skinners? – unthinkable – all she could do was protect and indicate, as subtly as possible, willingness to do battle.

The next morning Daisy took a telephone call.

Brenda barked, 'Miss Mannering.'

'I'm afraid she's not available.'

'Who's that?'

You know perfectly well who it is. 'Daisy.'

'What do you mean? Not available.'

'She's in the bath,' Daisy improvised.

'Get her to phone me when she's out.'

'She won't be able to. She has to leave immediately for a meeting —'

The phone slammed down.

She thought about not telling Floy, then decided she would have to, but not yet. She waited until the daily woman, Mrs Lowe, arrived and said, 'Would you mind, Mrs Lowe, Miss Mannering's resting. If anyone phones, would you mind asking who it is and saying she'll call back —'

'Anyone particular?' Mrs Lowe seldom wasted words.

Daisy thought for a moment. 'Er – Mrs Brenda Hutton.'

'Huh, them Skinners.'

No more needed to be said. As a child, Daisy had found Mrs Lowe intimidating and always played well out of her range. Time gradually revealed beneath the armoured exterior a woman with a strong sense of duty and a kind heart, unfailingly loyal to Floy, and as reticent in her own way as Floy. A great deal was understood between Daisy and Mrs Lowe.

In the early evening while they were enjoying their pre-dinner sherry under the pergola in the garden, Daisy said casually, 'Oh, Brenda phoned, earlier. But I didn't think it was anything much, so I said you were in the bath.'

Floy, with a sideways politely attentive nod, studied the blue flowered potato vine scrambling up and over the pergola. 'I always feel there's something – flirtatious – about *solanum crispum*. Would you agree?'

'You don't mind, do you, that I put her off?'

'I think it's an extremely good idea. Could I be in the bath next time she calls?'

'As often as you like.'

'Thank you, Daisy.'

Next day, in the hall, Daisy picked up the phone, said, 'Hallo? Hallo?' to a breathing silence.

The connection was cut. Oh, well, it happened.

But she stood looking malevolently down at the telephone. A Skinner?

It was all very well standing guard, if only she could do something to keep them away.

Something Daisy decided she could do for Floy was visit Hugh Stephenson. She did not say so to Floy, instead she left a note propped in the kitchen, saying she might pop in to the Manor Nursing Home while she was out. Conscience dealt with, she presented herself there later in the morning. The Manor was not without prestige, being in the seventeenth century a small residence – small by the standards of its time – when it had accommodated within its beautiful architecture family, extended relations, dependants, regular visitors, servants, outdoor staff…

And there, lulled by the sweep of its landscaped gardens, the elegant, expensively decorated reception area, expecting nothing except a casual visit, she was confronted by a barrier: a smartly dressed receptionist with a manner so devastatingly superior it was almost burlesque.

'You'll have to speak to Sister Wainwright.'

Sister, starched but human, with snub nose, thick glasses, wonderfully encompassing gaze, asked her – you don't mind? – to establish her identity. She explained why she was staying at Fairmead, her connection to the Mannerings, and the Mannerings' long connection with Hugh Stephenson. Then she had, amazingly, to produce a driving licence, documentation. 'You see,' Sister said, 'there's so much fraud now.'

How would anyone dare be anything but honest? Lie to this woman and you're out on your ear. Daisy found herself pulled up by a passage of time she would never have taken into account. Flitting everywhere with her mother, living in Ireland, England, Rhodesia, South Africa, it didn't matter where, how far she had travelled, geographically and in time, she was imbued with the values of suburbia, the bedrock of her childhood: its acceptance of who you were because of who you knew, its discretion, its trust. But somewhere, bewilderingly, these values had veered into avenues of deception and crime.

She was encouraged, and it became a pleasure, to talk of her many visits over the years to Bankhill, the Mannering family and friends, found, to her surprise, that she had told Sister about when she was a girl, and Quill took her hunting in the Cheshire Forest. Quill's sweet forbearance at her being so often thrown and landing upside down in ditches, suggesting gently, 'Darling, perhaps you should have HELP printed on the seat of your breeches.'

Sister said, 'Sir Aquilla, a gentleman of the old world.'

Yes, that just about summed up Quill.

'He was here just before Christmas, and I understand he's Mr Stephenson's oldest friend, his visits mean a great deal. And you think he might come soon?'

'He's hoping to. I haven't seen him for just over two years, I stayed with him in Ireland. He was rather frail.'

'I did notice that last time he was here, but he is still pretty mobile, isn't he? Mr Stephenson's visitors are few and far between.' She looked at Daisy with, it seemed, an enquiring gaze.

'Well, you'll know Hugh's been a widower for years. He never had any children, I don't know about any other family. Floy hasn't mentioned anyone. There are old friends, but they're either ill, or moved away. Floy would like to come, but it's difficult because of her operation, I'd be only too happy to bring her when she feels up to it.'

'So you're visiting on their behalf?' Sister smiled.

'Um, yes.' Daisy suddenly grasped the intention behind that nuanced smile: she had been allowed to talk so freely about inconsequentials to establish her credentials.

Sister said, 'People don't appreciate how fatiguing a stroke is. Mr Stephenson can't work at contact with newcomers. As you said yourself, there are so few connections left from his earlier years, scarcely anyone it seems. Unless you know, not necessarily personally, I mean, but know about…anyone?'

'Well, no…'

'No, you're far too young, all the old friends, intimates, business contacts have, sadly, died off. Any other visitors, presenting themselves, well, you see, Mr Stephenson was well known in the past, older people who might only have heard of his considerable reputation could be merely – inquisitive. If I have no way of assessing how genuine they are, I naturally exercise my own judgement.'

'Yes,' Daisy agreed, aware that she was missing something – but what?

Was she expected to pursue a hint so subtle? Or was it merely a continuance of Sister's breadth of knowledge of the everyday, of her care and protectiveness of ordinary comfort that filled Daisy with respectful amazement. 'Oh, do you mean I shouldn't, you'd rather I didn't —'

'Goodness, no. Do see him, there'd be nothing taxing about your presence, and you know people whose names he'll recognise. That will be a comfort to him,' Sister said with bracing kindness. 'As a matter of fact, I've been thinking, sitting here talking to you – he has many of his photographs around him – there's one of a young woman who could almost be you.'

'Oh, I must see if I recognise who it is. How is Mr Stephenson?'

'He made a significant recovery after his first stroke a year ago, but two of his old friends died within a short space and he became rather depressed, naturally enough. When Sir Aquilla comes he'll see a deterioration, I'm afraid. Mr Stephenson's speech isn't affected, but his memory is. He can't recollect anything before the stroke, and one side of his body is disabled, he's incontinent and there's some loss of visual field.'

'Oh, gosh. Poor man.' She took this in, Sister did not hurry her. 'I'm not sure it would be a good idea to encourage Floy to visit him.'

'You know best. She hasn't seen him since he was much more able, she could find it an ordeal. Anyway, think about it. Come along, I'll take you myself.'

Of course she would, nothing escaped Sister's vigilance – if Hugh had an adverse reaction to Daisy's presence, the visit would be no more than – *Hallo, how well you look* – and there's the door.

Chapter Six

His room gleamed with soft colours and bowls of flowers; there was a clinical stringency in the air, beneath which, something cloying...rotting. Everywhere, his own photographs: landscapes, buildings, loving portraits. Floy, at twenty? twenty-five? in the dining room at Fairmead, its heaviness of carved oak and tapestry contrasting with the gossamer of her youth. The trained posture, the nervously gentle smile. How beautiful she had been.

Golden youth – Clive and Edward as boys, turned towards each other, laughing, all the heedlessness, the promise. Her own mother (of course, the likeness to Daisy unmistakable) – young, radiant, indicating admiration in the beholder – something else? Could her mother and Hugh...? Well, she would never know, and now was not the time to ask. Quill, in his middle years, the fine-drawn gentleman, his sweet masculine beauty.

These photographs, these faces and bodies, surged with a sensual love of life, as if Hugh had escaped into a dimension beyond the polite restraints of the time when he recorded them and carried his sitters with him. Now their vibrant companionship guarded him as his existence ebbed away in confusion and indignity.

He sat upright, in a dressing gown of Noel Coward elegance – but he had been famous as a charmer. Daisy retrieved the memory of admiring observations, warnings of the enjoyably forbidden: *handsome as the devil.*

He smiled at her, nodding as she introduced herself, said, 'Ah yes —' on a lifting note of recognition. She said, 'You knew my mother —' indicating the photograph.

'Ah yes,' he said again, nodding, smiling.

It became obvious, through the fractured conversation, that he smiled and nodded at everything. After a while he became occasionally urgent, dry hand clutching her own. 'Where? Where is he?'

She cast about, tried 'Quill?' and produced a startlingly lucid moment, 'Quill's here. Let me see him, where?'

'Um, no, but he is going to visit you – is that what you'd like —'

'Where is he? I have to tell him, you know. Edward.'

'Um – yes.' A tugging at her wrist, *Sister Wainwright, where are you?*

'Clive. Don't believe him. Edward. I've kept it for Quill. Tell him.'

Then he leaned back, began a long monologue about someone called Cuthbert who had always done his best to take over the chairmanship. After a while she realised he was talking about Bankhill photographic club which, she recalled, his father had founded in the Thirties, he had subsequently taken over, and had become defunct in the Fifties. As far as he was concerned, the power struggle that involved a bewildering number of names was still unendingly playing itself out.

When she got up to leave, exhausted, he said with a clarity missing from his earlier remarks, 'Don't forget. Tell Quill. He's to listen. He stays in Ireland because he wants to keep away from it all, he always has. Tell him to come. It's important.' He clasped her arm again, twisting his head down and sideways; she remembered his vision was impaired, this was obviously the only way he could look into her eyes with disconcertingly iron intent. 'I've kept it. Safe.'

'Yes, I'll tell him. I promise.'

'But you see, it's Floy. She has to know. She was her sister. It's there, with Floy.'

At the reception desk the daunting receptionist was telling a subdued-looking elderly woman that it was 'quite out of the question, quite out of the question. You'll have to see Sister first, and she's at lunch. You may wait.'

She turned to Daisy with an air of extreme efficiency and unction, 'And how did you find Mr Stephenson?'

Sister knew where to look for him, I don't suppose he rattles around much. She said coolly, 'Quite well. I wanted to see Sister but if she's at lunch it'll wait till the next visit.'

'Oh, do, do come any time.' In the offensively fawning manner the reassurance that she had passed whatever test was necessary and won Sister's approval.

The best moment to tell Floy anything was during a quiet garden stroll.

Floy's love for her garden was possessive and personal, she had designed it, worked at it robustly in her younger days with wheelbarrow and spade, but had long since handed over the physical work to Mrs Lowe's husband.

Floy was pointing out the *phygellius*, so showy, such fun, '– and, Daisy, did you know *kniphofia* – red hot pokers – can be pale yellow? Lovely architectural plants. That one's called Percy's Pride, Irene bought it for me after our Uncle Percy died in Kenya. We were so fond of him, a lovely man.'

'Floy, I went to the Manor nursing home today to visit Hugh. I know you're not quite up to it yourself, and Quill would like news of him.'

'That was very considerate of you. And how was he?'

'Not very well, I'm afraid.' Gently as possible, she explained Hugh's condition.

Floy listened, contemplating a splendid *fatsia japonica*, murmured how sad, such a very attractive man… 'But you couldn't make sense of what he said?'

'No, living in the past, which seems to make sense to him.'

'I suppose he's happier there,' Floy said so quietly Daisy scarcely heard.

'He did have the odd lucid moment. He very much wants to see Quill. I promised he would. Do you think I did the right thing?'

'I'm sure you've done everything for the best,' Floy sounded disconcertingly as if she needed to be convinced. 'You'll have to tell Quill —'

'Oh, yes, don't worry. I'll get in touch with him.'

They walked on a little way. 'But I tell you what,' Daisy said. 'I had to be positively vetted before I got near him. Sister Wainwright guards her charges like a jungle mother.'

'She is very conscientious, but are you exaggerating, Daisy? Her patients, or residents or whatever pay a great deal to stay at the Manor. Surely they have a say in who they wish to visit them.'

'Of course, if they're capable. But really, Hugh isn't. I think she sees her charges as especially vulnerable when they're not well, and she won't have them upset.'

'Yes, yes, quite right. And that's very – reassuring.'

'I'll pop in and look at dinner. Would you like sherry out here?'

Floy gazed about. 'No, there's a slight chill, don't you think? Let's go indoors.'

During dinner, eating her usual sparrow's portion, Floy said, 'I am grateful to you, Daisy, but I feel so selfish sometimes. The way you look after me,' she paused, added absently, 'protect me.'

'I love it, you know that. And it's not for ever. People make terrific recoveries after hip operations. You'll probably take up roller skating. And I'll be off with Ellie, running the dancing school.' It was up to her to be positive. Some people never recovered properly, but she wasn't going to say that.

Chapter Seven

On a heavy, overcast day, Daisy drove Floy in Floy's Rover to a buffet lunch with friends, then an afternoon with the music appreciation group. 'You'd be so welcome,' Floy said, 'if you'd care to join in.'

'Thanks, sorry, no.' Peter Pears' energetic vocalism was the last thing Daisy wanted; she had a plan underway, a course of action.

Back at Fairmead, she let herself into the silent house, hurried through her carefully prepared arrangements, went out again. She had parked in the drive – thank God for the privacy of long gardens, shielding shrubberies and, on a grey, stuffy morning, no one out and about to dead-head roses, mow lawns.

Her knowledge of Chatfield was not exactly extensive, but she had refreshed her memory, scouting for two days, and come upon the right location. A dreary stretch off the main road, depressed and depressing. One street among many sad, shabby, depopulated streets: a bicycle shop, second hand furniture emporium, dry cleaners, waste ground littered with rubbish, an electrical repair shop, closed – everything seemed to be closed, apart from the bicycle shop with its outside display of captive, chained bicycles and the dispirited custom to and from a grubby corner off licence.

She parked between a Baptist chapel and a boarded-up laundry, got out. Walked smartly away.

In twenty minutes she was at her destination, New Talbot Way, Chatfield sub-divisional headquarters. 'My car's been stolen,' she said to the constable behind the desk.

She was directed to take a seat, waited, was shown to an interview room.

A plain, pleasant woman police constable introduced herself as PC Mary Clegg, and her colleague PC Brian Ferris. He was overweight and had a soundless suggestion of heavy breathing. His eyes, small and puffy in his large face, regarded her unblinkingly on a sideways gaze of riveted caution. She had a wildly unprompted thought: somewhere she'd read that elephants were afraid of mice...

She gave her name and address and circumstances: she was staying with Miss Floy Mannering of Fairmead, Palmerston Road, Bankhill. Miss Mannering was her mother's oldest friend and the stolen car belonged to her. It was a 1948 Rover 16. PC Clegg, scrupulously filling out a crime report, looked up. Really? That was a classic car, wasn't it? Daisy said yes.

Some subterranean physical surge indicated a connection in PC Ferris's synapses. 'That Rover. Doesn't she have anything more – up to date?'

'No,' Daisy said helpfully. 'You see, it was a present to her from her parents, when it was new, she's always loved it. Of course, it's not terribly convenient for long journeys or whatever. If she has to, now, then she just hires a car.'

PC Ferris, known as Brute Force for entirely justified reasons apart from his initials, mouthed Bloody Hell in recognition of a lifestyle so alien he could manage no audible response.

PC Clegg brought them back to the business in hand. 'And when was the car stolen?'

'This morning, I drove Miss Mannering to a meeting of her music group at Herbert Vale. And then, just after, it was stolen. I don't know the exact time. And, of course, Miss Mannering doesn't know anything about this. I came straight here. I don't want to distress her, you see, her health...'

'So it was stolen outside a house in Herbert Vale?'

'Oh, no. I left Floy – Miss Mannering – there and drove home alone to Fairmead.'

'Fairmead?' Brute Force questioned. He had been so engrossed looking at Daisy he had taken very little in so far.

PC Clegg sighed, she had worked with him too often. 'On Palmerston Road?'

'Yes. I left the car in the road because I was going out later. I did some things in the house, then I went out – and – the car had gone. I thought it might be a little farther down the road, so, I thought if I walked...it might be...'

PC Clegg leaned forward. 'Yes?'

'Somewhere…'

PC Ferris made a hoarse sound that didn't resolve itself into speech.

PC Clegg said, 'You walked because you thought the car might be… Somewhere.'

'Yes, that's right.'

After a pause PC Clegg said carefully, 'Wouldn't it have been more sensible to go back in the house and phone us?'

'Well, yes, it would. But, at the time… I've never had anything stolen, you see, and I was rather confused, so after I'd walked for a while and hadn't seen it anywhere, I thought I'd report it to you. By then, I was at the railway station, so I caught the train. Here.'

Toneless, PC Ferris stated, 'You must have seen someone in drive, heard car starting. Summat.'

'No. I left the car on the road outside. I couldn't see it from the house, there's a bend in the drive, and evergreens.'

'Evergreens,' he repeated.

There was a silence in which they both regarded her. She said diffidently, 'I thought, perhaps, if you went round, well, not exactly to Fairmead, but if you were seen in the Avenue, people might tell you things, if they'd seen anyone suspicious around.'

'Do they see owt round there?' PC Ferris asked.

Unoffended, Daisy said, 'Well, there was…'

They said, 'Yes?' in chorus.

'A prowler, no one knows who. Somebody…seen quite recently around the footpaths.'

'They ought to be done away with.' PC Ferris's robust view. 'All that – gardening. Straight roads with lighting, that's what's needed there.'

PC Clegg persevered. 'A man?'

'Er, yes, so I understand.'

She was asked had she seen him or could she give the names of anyone who had and could reply with honesty, if not accuracy, not really. Did she have any reason to believe that the prowler was linked to the theft of the car? Did Miss Mannering?

She said firmly, 'I haven't spoken of it to her, and no one else has. She's rather frail and nervous, I'd hate to alarm her, perhaps all over nothing.'

Brute Force said, 'Nuffin. Your car's taken and driven away, you've got a nutter on the prowl —'

'Miss Donovan,' Mary said, in the hope of stopping Brute Force. Could anyone? He was like a massive boulder bouncing downhill. 'What my colleague means is that if you feel there is something in your neighbourhood you think isn't quite right, we can give you assistance.'

Daisy said how kind and how much she appreciated their concern, and she would certainly contact them if...' Then she left.

She returned to Bankhill by train, a route preferred to car or bus. A branch of the main line from London to Holyhead pottered to Bankhill, the perfect station of gabled pavilions, diamond paned-windows, carved barge boarding, rescued from the 1840s when the Cheshire Lines Committee built their flawless, workaday stations. The platform gardens – winners of how many best-kept awards? – scrupulously tended by men who assumed nothing beyond the conscientiousness of their work and thanked their stars they had, for unknown reasons, escaped Beeching.

There was restoration work going on, the original footbridge of giddying height had been found unsound, its temporary replacement was a lengthy diversion. It never mattered to Daisy what pragmatic improvement or elaborate engineering the council proposed and the *Bankhill News* reported, to her this was always a version of the 1951 Emett railway: Far Twittering to Oyster Creek.

The festival of Britain occurred before she was born, but she had heard her mother, Floy and Quill talk about it, read about it, knew it in her bones as part of the warp and weft of Bankhill. Once, shortly after her operation, Floy, struggling and worn, murmured, 'I belong to a generation that is quietly slipping away into the outer darkness.' And Daisy, answering with love and yearning, said, 'Take me with you,' on an immediate vision of the railway lines running straight beneath the high bridge, through Bankhill station, leading from past to present.

She did not have to collect Floy (an arrangement she had taken advantage of for her own purpose). A friend would drive Floy home later and stay for dinner. She had scarcely got in when the phone rang. The caller was PC Mary Clegg. In spite of her polite briskness there was a suggestion of bafflement: the Rover had been found.

'Er, gosh. Super,' Daisy said; she had taken care to leave it in the general vicinity of the police station on the obscure assumption it would be safe and soon found. Even so. Perhaps that road was so completely uninteresting people were too bored to cause trouble.

'I put out a call to all local patrols to keep an eye out for it. One of our foot patrol radioed in just now. He's keeping an eye on it and making a few enquiries along the road, there could be an eye witness when it was abandoned.'

'How very,' Daisy said, so appalled she ran out of words.

'He'll wait for you to turn up and collect it.'

'That's – that's very kind of him.'

'Just doing his job. It wasn't exactly far away.'

'No, it wasn't – I mean *wasn't it?* Er – whereabouts…'

'Brick Road.'

'I didn't notice the name.'

'I beg your pardon, Miss Donovan?'

'I don't know – know – the names of many roads in Chatfield. Well, some, in the centre, but not on the outskirts.'

PC Clegg murmured, 'Did I say Brick Road was on the outskirts?'

Where had she heard that the only thing to do with foot-in-mouth was leave it there? 'Is the car all right?'

'All present and correct. Completely undamaged. Driveable.'

'Thank you. I'll get a taxi straight away.'

'We'll arrange for some house-to-house on Palmerston —'

'But it's found now, you wouldn't want to —'

'If there's a thief about we'd like to find out who he is. One of your neighbours could have seen a stranger acting, looking suspicious. And you did want a bit of a uniformed presence about the place, didn't you? To – er – discourage the prowler.' A hint of amusement.

Daisy had the sensation of being in a madly accelerating tumbrel – and it was her own fault for starting it. Now she had to think of what she could tell Floy when PC Clegg – worse – PC Ferris turned up on the doorstep and Palmerston Avenue seethed with policemen.

PC Clegg was explaining, '…most of us use that road on the way to and from work.'

'Ah,' Daisy said.

There followed an explanation: the change of shift. Patrols going out fresh with the immediate knowledge of a very noticeable stolen car. And there it was. On their doorstep. Who could miss it?

Who indeed?

Daisy put the phone down and her head in her hands.

A close-run thing? What?

Five minutes and they'd have caught her abandoning it.

Chapter Eight

Steadfastly undeterred, immediately on the return of Floy's car, she put into operation the next part of her plan, which made it necessary for her to pick through reluctant shreds of information about the habits of the Skinners, finally selecting the ceremonial occasion of Sunday dinner. This, she had come to understand, without in the least requiring the knowledge, was when the clan cohered.

So... An evening walk. Passing by. Call in...

Only when it was almost too late did she realise her mistake. A time confusion, a social gaffe. Dinner to them meant lunchtime to her. Lunchtime it would have to be. She readjusted her time scale, set out smartly at 11.30 for the good two mile walk.

Almost at her destination, she found roads feeding so insensibly between private and council housing it was impossible to disentangle which was which. This, she knew, was an area where Floy's next door neighbour owned whole streets of houses, let for rent, a circumstance common everywhere; the Mannerings themselves once, perhaps still, owned property here.

Her interested gaze found some houses shabby, neglected, others proudly cherished neat gardens, snowy curtains, scrubbed paintwork. Her destination, 14 Canal Road, was a fair-sized house on a corner with a segment of garden punished by generations of children: a bald lawn, drifts of wrecked toys, a collapsed corrugated iron – dog kennel? a clothes line with flapping contents.

The front door stood open, gusting out the sound of voices, cigarette smoke, cooking smells. She looked down a narrow hall, a stretch of scuffed linoleum, assorted footwear, coats bulging from pegs. She tried the bell, to no effect, if it rang anywhere no one heard it. She plied the knocker. A slender girl crossed the hall, glanced at her, passed on, then a smiling middle-aged woman appeared, 'Hallo, love, you from council?'

'What? Gosh, no.' She managed a muddled explanation, found that the word 'family' acted as an unlocking mechanism, taking her into a hectically carpeted room crammed with furniture and people, somewhere there was music from a wireless. Brenda appeared suddenly, dressy, coiffed to the last hair, insultingly polite, 'To what do we owe the honour?' turned away as Daisy said she was just having a morning walk and...

Brenda attached herself to a small, confidential circle, all of whom spoke low-voiced, turning to smirk at Daisy. Heads swivelled, voices seeped, Who? Oh, her...you mean...

Marooned, she swallowed fury. After all, she was not an invited guest. And there were not so many people, it just seemed as if...

'Hallo.' A small, sturdy boy stood before her, an immense slice of bread and dripping in his hand. It looked delicious. 'I'm little Bert. I'm eight.'

'Jolly good.'

'Yes. Can I get you anything. Drink of water?'

'Thanks, no. I'm fine.'

'Are you Aunt Florrie?'

Daisy said no, gently, aware of garbled explanations, sniggers from Brenda's coven. A generation separated her from Floy, but she smiled at little Bert's solemnity, when you were eight a difference of forty years was neither here nor there.

'Well,' he said, serious, 'Are you a teacher?'

'I teach dancing.'

He stared. Walked off with an outraged: 'Dancing's daft.'

Stared at, aware of whispers, Daisy attempted to circulate, encountered bewilderingly duplicate names – like little Bert, they all seemed to be named after one another: our Fred, our Ethel, young Nora, old Ben.

A Big John presented himself to her, she was sure he could have no relation to our John – who was mercifully absent, she would not have to endure his dumb gaze and superior family.

Big John: tall, heavy-set, thick dark hair, bandit moustache and kind brown eyes. Finding herself in a corner with him between a sideboard and an aspidistra stand was like washing up into a haven. He had an accepting air, world weariness and patience combined. He introduced himself, shook her hand, said in his deep, gentle voice, 'I'm trying to work it out, I think there's a –

well – by marriage connection. You see, your —'

Little Bert reappeared, steadying, 'Big John, *he's* all right.'

'Oh, thank you, little Bert,' Daisy said, aware of some protectiveness. 'I'm sure he is.'

'Yes, well, you can never tell. Some of them are right wankers,' he walked gravely away.

They exchanged a wordless look, smiling, then Big John reached out and drew forward a daughter, so much his own, heavy-set, raven-haired, easily smiling – Emma.

'Hallo, nice to meet you,' Emma said, punctiliously shaking her hand, and looking puzzled. 'But, I thought, someone – you're not Aunt Florrie's cleaner, are you?'

'Emma, where d'you get that idea?'

'Sorry, Dad, I didn't mean —'

'It's all right,' Daisy said quickly, wondering how much more she was to be downgraded, knowing it was not this polite young woman's fault. It belatedly occurred to her they were the only ones who had any physical contact with her; she was accustomed to the brushing cheek kiss, the caressing touch, the hug…but then – the thought of offering any of this to the Skinners was enough to make her run screaming. They would no doubt feel the same. 'Um… You see, she's my mother's oldest friend, she's had a hip replacement, and I'm helping her out until she's active again. But, her name…she's always called Floy.'

Emma considered this, said, oh, she didn't know, and it was a much prettier name, and she couldn't think how she'd got it all wrong.

'No, please,' Daisy murmured. 'Crossed wires. Happens in families.' Just about the last thing she meant to say.

Emma told her about how she was going to go to domestic science college in the autumn, said, 'Love the dress,' and went away.

Big John explained. Emma's mother – a Skinner, had left him for another man – they were divorced but he felt it his duty to see that Emma kept regular contact with her mother's family, she so much enjoyed the company of her cousins and aunts and uncles. Somehow he managed to hint that he didn't want his daughter to suffer for the mess her parents had made. 'They do really welcome her,' he said. 'For me, it's just a matter of toughing it out.'

Daisy, charmed by his frankness and relaxed manner into possible indiscretion said, 'I can't believe you're not popular.'

'Oh, I'm popular all right. Just no one likes me.'

She burst out laughing. 'I'm sure that's not true. I was about to commiserate with you. Fellow feeling. I'm certainly not popular.'

'Fellow feeling? What are you talking about? You're a lady.'

'God God, I'm not,' Daisy said faintly.

'Oh yes you are. It's nice you're here. But, why?'

Then she became aware of the silence spreading around them. Nobody, not even Brenda, knew the reason for her presence. She was the intruder, she didn't belong —

But now she was here, and she had to account for herself.

She would.

Faces turned towards her as if on a tide of rejection. Voices died. No one would say anything. She recognised that she had to, and made the most of it. She had purpose, and an audience.

Miss Mannering's car, she announced, had been stolen.

Somewhere, a male voice muttered, grieving, '*What, that Rover?*'

Yes, yes, taken from the drive, in broad daylight. Fortunately found undamaged. Returned. But then…there was the prowler.

The what? The who?

Goodness knows what his motive was. Seen in the neighbourhood, no definite recognition. She had not told Floy, of course, for fear of upsetting her.

Who? What? Floy? Who's Floy? Aunt Florrie. Oh…

'The police,' Daisy said firmly, 'are watching the place constantly, they're going to keep round-the-clock surveillance —'
The mad enjoyment of overplaying.

A hiatus into which slyness, uneasiness, seeped. Physical reaction: elbows nudged, glances turned away, words muttered. Yes, her intuition had been proved right.

Then in the breath-caught pause, Brenda snapped, 'I've not got time for this. We're going down pub.'

With a surge of concerted movement, indicating relief and long habit, the tide of Skinners retreated. Big John loomed, solid and comforting. 'Come along and have a drink.'

Her instinctive trust of him had become entangled with her bewilderment of the multiplicitous Skinners. (Well, the Mannerings could talk. Floy's father had been one of six brothers, all but one – Aquilla – married and enthusiastically breeding. You felt they were doing it on behalf of England, threading the name of Mannering through the warp and weft of the British Empire.)

But she was diverted by practicalities. If they're all going 'down pub', who on earth would cook lunch? She did a rapid sweep, came up with a whining old aunt, many aggressive children, a sweet-faced woman in a wheelchair who plainly wasn't going to do anything, anywhere.

'What?' Big John asked.

'Who's seeing to lunch?' she said, low voiced.

He put his hand on hers for a moment, a large hand, thickly padded, capable, conveying he understood and forgave. 'Dinner,' he murmured, 'that's what we have here. Not lunch.'

'Oh, yes. Sorry.'

'The grandparents, family tradition. They see to it. You've not met them?'

'Um…' Who had she met? Or not?

Somebody returned from the exodus, grabbed the wheelchair and trundled the sweet-faced woman away. She gave a smile and a wave to Daisy.

'Come on,' Big John said. He took her through the hallway to the back of the house, a large kitchen with crazed white tiles, obscured glass windows and a deep ceramic sink fed by visible pipework. A square oilcloth covered table, set with cutlery for eight, sauce bottles, a large cruet, cups and saucers, took up almost all the space, they had to squeeze round it.

Stolidly at work a tall, thin man and a short thin woman basted roast lamb on the continuum of chopping mint, arranging roast potatoes, preparing vegetables. Big John said in a quiet, friendly way, 'Grandparents – I don't think you've met Daisy. Daisy Donovan.' He explained her, and then accounted for her, 'She's, well, sort of family.'

They did not answer or look at her, made nodding motions and gestures that conveyed they were too occupied with important matters to be bothered. Their clothes had an old, cared-for look, their shoes shone. Time had worn them down, striving, to an unassailable respectability.

'Hallo, how are you?' Daisy said brightly, aware that she was under an obligation to be polite.

Mrs Skinner made a sound like 'Humph,' and shook her head.

Big John said, 'Did you hear about Miss Mannering's car being stolen…' and Daisy knew they knew who she was, just as they had been told the entire story of the car because since her arrival every word she had spoken had been repeated – and she knew that *he* knew that and for her sake was trying to wring some response from them. They had every right to resent her as uninvited, but her lifelong reflexes dictated: a stranger in one's house was treated with minimal courtesy. This sense of reciprocal good manners foundered on their undisguised rejection of her. *What had she ever done?*

From the sink, Grandmother Skinner said shortly that them as is fortunate enough to own a car can expect anything.

Daisy tried to make sense of this.

Grandfather was nodding strenuously. He was not wearing his teeth, they reposed in a glass on the window ledge, contributing their own ferocious conversation. Daisy had an unbidden reprise of Floy's reference to them: forbidding, unfeeling. Yes, and the rest.

She made a last try, floundering on the past, so much of which, she suddenly realised, was unknowable to her; the friendship between her mother and Floy went back before she was born. She stammered explanations to faces turned away, offering into the hard silence anything she could think of —

Irene – and Stanley —

'Knew them, did you?' Grandfather asked over his shoulder.

'Well, no, I was only about – four, I think, when Irene – um –

the accident – but, of course, when I used to stay, later on, Floy and Quill talked about them – and of course there was Clive's friend, your grandson, Edward.'

Wordless, impassive, they discarded their mundane activity and turned towards her on the transforming name. Somewhere in the workaday room, there was a breath of the exotic, the cherished. Their gaze darted towards her and away. She had no idea what the silence would bring until their questions began: how? where? framed awkwardly, on an edge of rancour, as if they resented her knowing him.

Unable to supply more than brief memories of childhood, she murmured some half fictions, 'And then, last autumn, I went to stay with Aquilla, in Ireland. And of course, Edward was there —'

Why of course?

'— for the hunting, he loves that —' Craven, more fiction in the face of leechlike attention, 'Yes, such fun, um, Edward's a superb rider —'

And selfish, a thruster, overriding hounds, never known to open or close a gate for anyone.

They nodded in satisfaction, as if his prowess was only to be expected, and derived entirely from them.

When she had faltered to a halt, they prompted her with remarks spoken over the shoulder that were not questions but required answers. He'd have had a bit to say for himself. Trust our Edward to be always going on about family. Can't get him to shut up. How often have we heard him say he thinks the world of us.

What could she answer before such unexpressed yearning? They were searching for validation of their worth from a man who – if he mentioned it at all – had nothing but contempt for his own background.

A direct question thrust itself into her mental fumbling. Grandfather: 'And what about him as is in the Manor?

Him? Manor? Him? Oh, Hugh… A missed context. What about him?

The old man's toothless smile was undisguised malice, but he turned away from her bewilderment, shrugging, leaving her to flounder. And then Grandmother began in a ludicrous sing song voice, her head nodding in time, 'Oh, Hugh. Him. Yes, him. And his *rep-u-tation*. We all know about that, don't we?'

Daisy had a blankness of being in unknown terrain, a single word anchoring her to sanity. Reputation. And, bizarrely, in this circumstance, Sister Wainwright. In Sister Wainwright's world Hugh's reputation had the weight of respect; here, where the fury of class operated, reputation had the stamp of censure, besmirched privilege. But why besmirched?

Before she could collect herself, speak, Grandfather rasped, 'And is that Sir Whatsit coming to see him or isn't he?'

'I – er – I don't...'

Grandmother took up her childish sing song, making puppet movements, 'Oh, she don't, she don't, no, she don't,' and then, on a dismissive sneer, 'No, they wouldn't tell her nothing, anyway, she's nobody.'

Daisy dared not look at Big John, the shame of witnessing the double act of these two old people to belittle and humiliate her was not her burden alone, they were his ex in-laws, his daughter's grandparents. She had taken the full force of their aggression, could not, in the scalding embarrassment of the moment account for it. She gave Big John a sideways look, *for Christ's sake rescue me.*

Chapter Ten

They left, her head ringing (*the family, the family*. Bloody Mafia), walked down the hall into the hot afternoon. There were no words to refer to the meanness, not of circumstance, but of mind. On the road ahead relatives swarmed, going down pub – or wherever their concerns took them. Two or three or four stood close together at gateways or corners, talking in low voices, calling raucously to Big John. 'All right? Gerrup there. What about your Josie?'

They had used up all their embarrassment in the kitchen, this was nothing, easy to ignore, just men who shouted incomprehensible remarks and laughed at unknowable jokes.

'Sure you won't come and have a drink,' Big John said quietly. 'If you don't fancy the crowd, we could go somewhere else.'

'Thanks, no…um, that's nice of you, but…'

'Well, as you're going this way.'

They walked together; he said, 'I've seen Miss Mannering – before her op – driving about in that Rover. Perfect match, aren't they? Elegant, classy. They're smashing cars, that lovely deep green. What's it like to drive?'

Only too thankful to grasp at the ordinary, Daisy considered the masculine worship of anything with wheels and an engine. She felt quite inadequate to live up to his evident admiration, she could scarcely say she would rather have a modern car, so she made do with something inadequate about it being a joy and comfortable. It was her day for half truths and varnished lies, but she could at least say honestly that what she really loved was the sight of the Viking Warrior figurehead on the bonnet, the wings of his helmet streaming, road conquering, unquenchable.

'D'you ever operate the free-wheel device? You'd have to be careful not to in town, you haven't got so much control have you? What's it like?'

'Yes. It saves fuel. No, I only use it on clear roads – a bit like coasting downhill on a bike. Super.'

'I've seen Clive driving it sometimes.'

It was Clive who had restored it, still looked upon it as a spoiled darling. 'Do you know each other?'

'Well, only in a nodding sort of way.'

She asked, 'This um, family Sunday tradition. But...there are so many people, I mean, the kitchen, it's not...'

He explained complicated arrangements in his unruffled way. Only eight could be seated for Sunday dinner, participation was by rote, those not included went to their nearby homes for tea and gossip, went down pub, or followed their own interests. It was an enduring ceremony, with links to every age level, every generation and condition, Emma was at that moment off with several of her cousins.

Daisy, survivor of a dislocated childhood, felt a fleeting envy. She had never known her father, who had left her mother six months into their marriage, before Daisy was born. She was reconciled to having no relatives on his side, few on her own. As a child she had fantasised about belonging to the Mannerings – or any large family that chance threw up. But her envy could not survive the reality of this rude, purblind family, and Big John's easy acceptance of it made her rash, indiscreet. 'They hate me, don't they? Most of them have never seen me till today. But they hate me. And dear Floy. What has she ever done to hurt them?'

They walked a few paces, then he said, 'There's a sliding scale of resentment. You, the Mannerings, are right at the top. I'm lower down, but you see, I'm related to Edward's father, Stanley.'

'Edward's – oh, the Stanley who married Irene. I didn't know either of them. They both died in the same year, didn't they? Sad. Floy always says what a lovely man he was. How are you related?'

'He was my uncle. He came from a solid, craftsman's family. When he married Irene he was shoved into the category of people with "side".'

Side. Yes, she knew about that. *How* she knew was lost in the labyrinth of suburban social degrees. Side meant you aspired to something you were not, put on airs, assumed gentility in voice and manner.

But then she retrieved from family lore a Stanley sweet and calm, whose short marriage to Irene was a joyful fulfilment to them both. And there were photographs, hands clasped, loving smiles… It was cruel to make such a derogatory judgement – *side* – after they had both died and could not speak of how much they had meant to each other.

'Your uncle – are you like him?'

A gust of laughter. 'No, he was a whippet, not a lump like me.'

He was a lump, so was his daughter. But they were nice lumps, friendly and accepting, he was so easy to be with she realised in a light-headed way they were talking of personal matters on the merest acquaintance.

She asked him if he was a craftsman, he said no, he was in business, central heating, then reverted to the Skinners. 'The grandparents had to struggle, they're proud of their worth as hard workers. Grandfather served out his time as a council employee. Grandmother worked as a cleaner.'

She retreated to careful generality, 'Women of her generation, with no educational opportunities, what else could they do?'

'Yeah. She left school when she was fourteen, had her first child ten months after marriage at eighteen.'

At least he took the trouble to know about them, to interest himself in the facts of their lives – even with the excuse of being related she could have done neither, her instinct was to stay as far away from and forget as much as possible about such unpleasant people. She said something inadequate about social expectations and changing behaviour.

His voice was amused, ironic. 'Do you know why they've no time for posh types like you?'

'Even if I was, but I'm not, I'm not going to apologise.'

'Why should you? I should, though.'

'You've lost me.'

'My girlfriend, Josie, owns the florist's shop at the Quadrant.'

'Well, you don't get much posher than that. I remember Josie Twemlowe from the tennis club, I didn't really know her. Do they still live on Balmoral Drive? Floy knew her mum, slightly, years ago. But I suppose Josie's married now.'

'Divorced. You said it. Balmoral Drive. Makes me a class traitor.'

She halted, studied him. 'Somehow I know you're not having me on.'

They resumed walking. 'One of Grandmother's jobs up till the Seventies, Eighties, was on Balmoral Drive, a lady professor. She was immensely proud of that, gave her status above other cleaning ladies.'

'You mean like Victorian servants doing one-upmanship below stairs.'

'Yeah. But how dare I now, working class lad, shack up with —'

'Oh, John, stop it. You're giving me a headache. I don't understand all this class business.'

'I do. I'm imprinted.'

She had to laugh at that. 'Like geese.'

'Just like geese. But don't dismiss it, Daisy, it can be killing.'

'This conversation's getting like a cul-de-sac. What about you and Josie, then. Super. Does her mum still live on Balmoral Drive?'

'Till just recently. She's gone into a nursing home, dementia.'

'Oh, that's sad.'

'Mm. Sad, and stressful. Josie's having to sort out all her effects. She had piles of stuff, wouldn't throw anything away – not household; she's not bothered about that, but diaries, letters.'

'Personal stuff.'

'And family, Mrs Twemlowe set such store by it. Both her and Mr Twemlowe's family lived here for generations, since before Bankhill was thought of. They were farmers, innkeepers, clockmakers, Mrs Twemlowe's got the lot, letters, bills, cuttings. Then when they married and moved to Bankhill in the Twenties, Mrs Twemlowe kept a diary about her doings, and Bankhill in all its stages from the Thirties right till, well just lately. Josie feels she ought to keep them, she takes things to show her, sometimes she seems to recognise a photo or something, but she doesn't really, just rambles on, poor old girl. Just a minute, here —'

They had come to a corner where a road called Arthur (who could he have been?) turned at a right angle. Big John indicated the garden of the house that stood at the triangular plot. The house itself non-descript, the garden ferociously ordered: slabbed paths patrolling rigid rows of vegetables in rich earth, not a weed dared show itself, much less the frivolity of a flower. He said, 'The grandparents, this is their house.'

Yes, it would be: the cultivation of how many years, the necessary frugality through decades of feeding themselves, their children and now, every Sunday they would walk down the road to their daughter's house, carrying cabbages and peas, parsnips and sprouts in supermarket bags.

Daisy said, 'Clive – Floy's nephew, he makes a living from stuff he won't throw away.'

'Oh, yes, he's the publisher, isn't he – I didn't make the connection. I like his books.'

'So do I.'

They stood at the literal parting of the ways. She was oriented to Bankhill, he and his sweet daughter to a life she couldn't know. Josie was lucky to have such a loving and understanding man. They shook hands. She said, 'I'm sorry, I've not behaved well at all.'

'Oh, yes you have, Daisy Donovan. They gave you a rough ride, you didn't deserve it. You could have smashed ornaments and shouted insults. But you didn't.' Said with an air of comprehensive acceptance of all the aberrations of human behaviour.

'Well, um,' confessional, 'I have – er – you know, on occasion. Smashed ornaments and...'

'Haven't we all.'

They shook hands, smiled goodbye. She walked away, thought of his decency, his unobtrusive male admiration, his insight into the complexity of family dynamics.

They had neither of them spoken of Edward.

And here was the mental entanglement – the grandparents' helpless adulation of Edward, their worn respectability – and her last visit to Ireland, which she had been forced to dissemble for their sake; the fear that in their hostility they had trespassed, reduced, distorted the best of it. But when she let her mind go she was swept into smudgy, lyrical winter days; the elegance of Quill's outworn country house; treasured servants, welcoming neighbours. Manners, customs, allegiances that now had no more than a finger-hold in England, died on elegiac whispers in Ireland.

An intermittent visitor since childhood, she had always suspected there was something magic and hidden in Uncle Quill's ivory tower life, and when she went back the last time – it was almost just the same. Only now there was Edward, a fixture.

A hunting morning trembled with the foretaste of hazard. Aquilla was then too frail to ride, he saw them off, kissing Daisy's hand and then, in homage to his male perfection and heaven knew what else, without reticence, touching Edward's mouth with his own, speaking words too soft for her to hear. When Edward turned away, dismissive to the point of contempt, Daisy saw clearly Aquilla's misplaced trust.

But then the memories unfurled, unstoppable: the ardent scent of churned loam, polished leather, horse sweat. Extraordinary, the smell of the riders, so pampered, rich, signature of the luxuriant aromas of the morning bath seeping into the racing, pressured day. A day of radiant faces, trembling hands lighting the last cigarette – (will it be the last? Is this to be death in the morning?), of heart-lurching hush when the covert is drawn.

Sepia and subfusc, the clods of flying turf; oh, God, the twilight of a hunting day, lowering mulberry light, weeping trees. And then, suddenly, after the kill – they'd gone, the whole boiling of them. Confusion. Thank God she wasn't alone. As always only one companion in the deserted landscape, Aquilla's neighbour, Lady Eleanor O'Flaherty. 'Where are we?' Eleanor's unerring sense of direction, 'We go this way,' firmly, a hieratic sweep of her riding crop. Great queens of Ireland in the past were so bold.

And then you were drinking in the pub. Outside, your horse, your warrior, mired, sound – thank all the pagan gods who care for their creatures – has a bucket of warm water with a pint of Guinness poured in…

Then the other memories trampled, obtrusive, unwanted.

Of Edward. The shit.

Chapter Eleven

In the luminous dusk of a summer evening, Detective Chief Inspector Sheldon Hunter drove through the outflung suburb of Bankhill, just about the most soothing area anyone could pass through to, eventually, reach Chatfield.

It was so far from his own background, his earliest years on a street-fighting Chatfield estate, he could have fallen in from another dimension. Later resentfully transferred to his uncle's house (willed to his mother) in a suburb of featureless gentility, he acquired an education – when he was too young to make any sense of it – in the gradations of class, the burden of those found wanting, the superiority of the fortunate.

But, that tranquil evening when he was driving along Palmerston Avenue, he saw a ghost.

She walked towards him in the massively gathering shade of laurels and rhododendrons – striding, elegant, full of grace, printing herself upon his amazed perception.

Her dress, fluidly caressing her dancer's body, of some delicate material that existed long before any notion of nylon or polyester was of the palest blue? green? The flouncing flare of its hemline stopped closer to ankle than knee; there was a scarf somewhere, lifting and trailing as she moved. Her light coloured shoes had Louis heels and bar fastening. Her hair, thick, dark gold, was cut in a little girl bob, caught back by a jewelled slide. Everything about her whispered privilege and leisure.

It was the first time in his trammelled existence that anything transcendental had ever happened to him and it was over in the breath of a sigh, vanishing, as he blinked.

He drew up, fell out of his car, looked back through the glimmering ranges of shrubs.

She was nowhere in sight.

Of course not. She was a dream, a manifestation of the past, an entity who, with the passion of her presence, somehow lingered on in the modernity of Bankhill.

He knew what he had seen, he knew it was impossible he could have taken in so many fine details on an instant, oblique glance. And when he thought about it afterwards he recognised his personal memory did not go back far enough to contain such perfect 1930s detail...

But how often had he stoically cleared out the houses of ancient aunts and uncles – the family albums, the hoarded newspapers and magazines. Those old hands, relinquishing their grip on the past, handed on to him a world, a life, and he had received, insensibly, the essence of this past. Years later, his knowledge was buttressed by further education, radio programmes, television, so that in spite of his background being completely at odds with the affluence of Bankhill, there had always been a surrounding sense of it: exclusivity, reticence, stability.

Its solidity was all around him in bricks and mortar, the cherished vernacular: criss-crossed oak beams, diamond paned windows, gables, balconies, spreading gardens tended for fifty years. And here and there, the architectural frivolity of the grandiosely named *moderne*: flat-roofed, white-painted houses, their sharp corners rounded by metal window frames.

All his life he had accepted it for what it was – a world created by and for a bygone middle class, neither town nor country, a tamed arcadia.

But now it occurred to him that beyond its reality there was a gradual alluring: heavy-headed trees, spreading shrubs, twisting roads, glimpses of a rooftop, a curving drive, a gateway. Suburbia was not virtuous, it was a concealment of the unmannerly, the reckless, the unforgiving sins. This insight seemed to him an aberration, he was tired, his senses momentarily disordered by the glimpse of her.

In his work he knew how appearance denied reality. It could, therefore, cautiously be said that if there were ghosts anywhere in the vicinity of Chatfield, they would be here, in Bankhill, moving through the overarching trees, the secretly stealing footpaths. He drove around, uselessly, helplessly, then at last went home.

He would never, in his workaday world, tell anyone about his ghost, but when he did win some leisure from his pressurised existence he diverted himself by gathering and reading anything he could find on Bankhill. And he had to admit he would never have given time for any of it but for his ghost.

The interior of his car was on the same scale of violent untidiness as his desk. Amidst God knew what, there were always books and it was DC Annette Jones who found them when they were driving from Talbot Way one day. Tall, gainly Annette Jones, raven-haired and rose-complexioned, was one of the best men on his team. When he first said that she whooped, delighted. She was ambitious, tough and intuitive, knew perfectly well how to respect their professional and private territories, but put her in sight of a book and her hands went out, a Pavlovian reflex he understood on his own behalf – how could he blame her?

She fell on a history of Bankhill. 'Love it, love it, there's so much there now still untouched, still in its own time capsule. My grandparents lived there.'

'Did they?' From what he knew of her background there was nothing surprising in that.

'Yes, they moved there in the Twenties, as newly-weds, it was still being built. And this publishing firm – you should have seen the stuff it was turning out then, and in my parents' time, real starchy. But it was taken over a few years ago, he does Chatfield too, and everything, where to eat and drink, where to disco, gay bars. God knows what my grandparents would have made of it if they'd lived long enough. In the Thirties, my grandmother had a Madam shop at the Quadrant.'

'A madam… Good God.'

'Hey, come on, guv. Madam meant something *quite* different then. Do you think I come from a long line of procuresses?'

'Well, you might.'

'No, listen. Up until the second world war, there were these – and this is what they were called – Madam shops. They were owned by trained dressmakers, they sold very good quality and ready made clothes, Molyneux, Norman Hartnell, whatever. Or they designed and made to order, which is what my Grandma did. Funny, not long since I found out James's old auntie used to buy from her —'

DS James Collier, Annette's ideal colleague, they shared the same age, background, ambition. She was slightly the taller, even in flat heels, like an older sister watching out for her brother, the fair-haired, scrubbed head boy of a very good school. In reality it was difficult to choose the tougher of the two, depending on the situation, how much force or cunning was required. Hunter's first instinct to team them together had proved consistently right – it could almost be said it was a marriage made in heaven, except that it was purely professional and devoid of emotional complication: Annette was intensely interested in men. So was James.

Having taken on board the Madam shops, Hunter said, 'So James has connections to Bankhill, as well?'

'Course, guv. We're Cheshire folk, like you.'

Good God, nothing like him. There reeled before him their social privilege, education, cushioned certainty – his street-fighting youth, his mother's hard-pressed, inventive house-keeping.

He drew into the car park at Talbot Way, said, 'Come on, don't let's hang around. Half past ten and the whippet's still in his nightie.'

'Yes, guv,' she agreed. It was five p.m. and there wasn't a whippet in sight. She was accustomed to him planting obscure observations into everyday exchanges, they unnerved many people, but she had come to recognise that he was somehow sustained by conversations going on inside his head. It was her private opinion that occasionally voicing them kept him sane.

Anyone who understood this in some way was at ease with him, had their favourite. Hers was, 'The sewing circle, and drive like hell.' For James it had always been, 'Children of the night, what music they make,' until someone heard it in an old Dracula film. By the unwritten rules of the game anything attributable was automatically disqualified. So James was waiting for a replacement.

And then there were the Frog and Nightgowns. When Hunter relaxed it was into the social companionship, the ease of good solid furniture, the rustle of newspapers, muted conversations, decent ale – no juke box, no muzak, no karaoke. The name of the pub was irrelevant, if it met these specifics, it was a Frog and Nightgown. And that was it.

Annette and James painstakingly tracked every one. Like Hunter they were freebooting, focussed on their work, any relaxation they could share with him was a bonus; on any given night they were reasonably sure where to find him. There was a scale of excellence, top of it the One Eyed Rat in Clerehaven; modest wooden floor, comfortable settles, and painted on the whitewashed wall the words, 'In the country of blind mice, the one-eyed rat is king.'

It had always been difficult to talk to Floy about personal matters. Apart from the strait-jacket tradition of reserve Floy, the nervous youngest sister, had always been protected; her sensitivity, her delicate health, demanded that she be shielded from unpleasantness. This was what her parents wanted, it justified their guardianship of her, confirmed their moral status. People just didn't confront Floy with anything nasty, the truth was that no one would have dared try it anyway when Irene was there, tough, capable, always ready to spring to her defence. Which made Irene's marriage a kind of defection, although Floy would never say so – and Irene was still there, vigilant…but then her death, so unexpected, deprived the little sister completely.

Sometimes it amazed Daisy that Floy had survived, but then, she had the sustaining influence of the rest of the family, long-established friends, a tradition of duty, of not giving way to adversity. All this compounded the sense of matters hovering, unsaid… Buried deep in Daisy was the fear that if she broke the tradition with too much questioning, too much directness, she might come upon some reckless knowledge and not know what to do with it.

And now, she found it impossible to tell her the truth about abandoning the Rover, the subsequent visit to the Skinners. Guiltily aware of being deceitful and taking the coward's way out – if she had confessed and Floy asked, *What on earth did you do that for?* she could only answer, 'To protect you.' And that sounded melodramatic and impertinent.

Floy's distraction had given way to something more relaxed, but still, there was a general atmosphere of strain. Daisy wished the next door neighbour was home; Floy's friend for forty years, Grace Wilmot was a woman very like Floy but with a broader experience of life. She had been a receptionist at her father's surgery, married, brought up children, was widowed, all of which gave her a robust approach to the world. She was away – forever, Daisy thought glumly – visiting her daughter in South Africa.

Not that it would have been possible to give or exchange confidences about Floy, but Grace's sensible presence would have been a help, and if it came to anything extreme (what?) Floy would have someone trusted close by.

Meanwhile, she had to talk to somebody, and there was only one person. She took herself off to Clive's firm in Chatfield.

Overlooking a garden square that was still a garden and had not been vandalised into a car park, the building, an escapee from the seventeenth century, had once housed the long defunct *Chatfield Courier*; fading letters on the old brick of the upper storey announced 'List of Visitors. Wednesday.'

His smile, his hug, greeted her apologetic, 'Sorry if you're busy, I'll go if I'm in the way.'

'Perfect timing, early lunch. Come on.'

When they were in Alistair's, currently his favourite bistro in the brick vaulted cellars of an old warehouse, she said, 'When I tell you, you might make me pay for my own lunch.'

'Right. What have you been up to, Dado?'

'It's difficult to know where to start.'

'What about the Rover.'

She spluttered wine. 'How do you…?'

'There was obviously something dodgy about that story. I didn't say as much to Floy.' Of course not, he was under the same constraint as herself, interactive speechlessness, discretion gone mad.

When she had told him, he gazed at her in disbelief. 'You *pretended* the Rover was stolen —'

'I know it's your baby. We got it back —'

'And invented a prowler —'

'I didn't tell Floy *that*, I'm not completely —'

'I don't know why the police didn't lock you up. I don't know how they could have *believed* you.'

'Well, um, perhaps they… Anyway, it worked.'

'What did?'

'It brought the police round to Palmerston Avenue in strength, knocking on doors, asking questions. Cars, uniforms. I tucked Floy well out of the way indoors – you know it's impossible to see or hear what's going on past those evergreens. Swore Mrs Lowe to secrecy'

He put his hand to his forehead. 'Daisy, have I missed something?'

'It's kept them away. The Skinners. I told you how much they upset Floy last time —'

'They've not been round again?'

'No...but Brenda phoned. I wouldn't let her speak to Floy. Then next day someone rang up and didn't say anything. I'm sure it was her.'

'Did you let her know that?'

'How? The last thing I wanted was a conversation with her.'

'Yes... You could have blown a raspberry.'

'Doesn't work over the phone, sounds like an inadvertent fart. The thing is, they don't like the police, I noticed it when Brenda was talking to John. I'm sure they've got criminal connections, or something. Anyway, I acted on the assumption they had. I went round to their house last Sunday lunchtime, because I knew lots of them would be there...'

'You went —'

'Shut up.' She explained what had happened. '...And when I told them about the police, there was a distinct frisson. And no, I haven't told Floy about that at all, I don't think she'd want to know.'

He said helplessly, 'Dado, this makes sense to you?'

'Yes, of course.'

'You really have been harebrained. You shouldn't mess with people like the Skinners, they can get nasty if you just look at them the wrong way. Leave them to themselves.'

Which was what he always did anyway, managing to ignore their existence.

'Is there anything else you've done that I should know about in case Floy asks me and I can say you haven't.'

'Not fair.'

'True.'

'Floy just didn't seem to want to go and see Hugh Stephenson. So I did.'

'Well, that was decent of you. How was the old boy?'

'Lost the use of one side of his body. Confused. His speech is clear enough but he rambles, talks about things that happened years, years ago, as if it's now. He mentioned you. And Edward.'

'What did he say?'

'Nothing, that was it, just once, your names. Nothing that made sense. But he is insistent on seeing Quill.'

'Did you phone Quill?'

'No, I wrote to him. I didn't want to —' She stopped just in time, took a sip of wine.

Didn't want to have to talk to bloody Edward. Delicate ground, for all sorts of reasons, only one of which was the awareness of a once more than close friendship. Another was an episode she had not spoken of to anyone, and if she ever did, it certainly wouldn't be to Clive. Clive's lack of interest in Edward was evident, when – seldom – he mentioned him, it was too casually to encourage response.

Daisy explained she hadn't wanted to get tangled up in that insane telephone system. 'I told Floy. She asked politely enough about Hugh, but she doesn't seem much concerned, hasn't mentioned anything about him since.'

He gazed at her thoughtfully. 'So. What Daisy Did Next.'

'Absolutely nothing. Can we change the subject?'

They talked of other things, eventually about Bankhill memorabilia. Daisy told him about meeting Big John at the Skinners'.

He groaned, 'Daisy, you're not collecting strays from that bloody family.'

'No, he isn't. Stanley Crane was his uncle. Big John's wife – *ex-wife* is a Skinner, she left him. He's got a girl friend, Josie used to be Twemlowe.'

'The Twemlowes who live on Balmoral?'

'Mrs Twemlowe still owns the house, but she's in a home.' Daisy told him about her collection of family papers. 'Might this be the next Bankhill memoir?'

Clive considered, he was, after all, a businessman, and this wasn't second- or third-hand, Uncle-Albert-used-to-say stuff.

'OK, it's your personal contact, if Josie agrees.'

'I'm sure she will. She doesn't give a damn about the stuff herself but she's got a conscience about hanging on to it, I think she'll be jolly glad to pass it over to a respectable custodian.'

'I've never thought of myself as a respectable custard. Next time you see your Big John, or Josie, you can ask. And have a glance at it yourself first, see what you think.'

In the late afternoon, Hunter and Mary Clegg drove back to Talbot Way sub-division headquarters after a difficult interview with a woman who had made a complaint against the police. Normally, Hunter would have taken Annette, but she was tied up with a rape case, half CID were at court, the rest were on a drugs operation. His second choice of Mary Clegg was deliberate; she was steady, sensible as a thermal vest, could be trusted in volatile situations, and was longing to be transferred to CID.

As they approached the sign indicating Bankhill, Mary asked hesitantly if he thought it was a funny place.

'Funny?'

'Oh, I don't mean as laughing, I mean – strange.' The least imaginative woman to wear a uniform, which was not to say she was without sensitivity and had sympathy in abundance, but she had to struggle with anything nuanced. 'I suppose I mean the residents. When all you've known is security and affluence and um —' she cast about for a word, 'discretion, I suppose you can sort of get left behind by the modern world. They just don't seem to expect to see police about the place.'

'They're bloody lucky they don't.'

'I didn't mean —'

'I know, it's not exactly a crime hot-spot. What you mean is – they can all be quietly mad and no one notices.'

'In an unthreatening way. For instance, last week we had a report of a stolen car from round here, a 1948 Rover 16.'

'A 19— are you sure you weren't caught in a time warp?'

'I did wonder for a minute. Belongs to a Miss Mannering. Palmerston Avenue.'

Palmerston Avenue. A whisper. A ghost. Now…a phantom car?

'Guv?'

'Nothing. Is that,' he said, deliberately plonking, 'Mannering as spelt Mainwaring?'

'Um, no, sir,' she said, bewilderment overtaken by suppressed panic. Was this one of his famously impenetrable non-sequiturs on which, it was alleged, people's careers had been known to crash for lack of savvy?

'You surprise me,' he murmured. So many households in Bankhill were inhabited by vocally incognito families: Marjoribanks – Marshbanks; Cholmondeley – Chumley. The occasional unadorned Blenkinsop came as a positive relief. Now he could add Mannering.

'We recovered it. It'd been abandoned in Brick Street. It was perfectly all right. But, tell the truth, guv, I've never come across anything so peculiar.'

'Tell me about it.'

From the concise details the picture emerged of an unremarkable incident; Mary gathering all the information she needed to initiate an investigation, passing it on to the local patrols; the recovery of the vehicle in less than an hour.

'That seems pretty straightforward,' Hunter said cautiously, knowing it couldn't be. Mary was a stranger to exaggeration, if she said it was peculiar it must have been.

'It was a young woman reported it. About thirty – and a bit dotty. Oh, she was really nice and – her clothes – and her figure —' The pauses were eloquent: the innocent envy of a plain, dumpy woman for unattainable glamour. 'But she wasn't telling the truth. I know she wasn't. PC Ferris said I was imagining things, but it's typical of Brute Force to dismiss her as —' Too late, she tried to gulp back the name. 'I mean, his assessment —'

'Mary, don't bother,' Hunter said kindly. Ferris was notorious for his pit bull instincts, which was a good reason for everyone to be wary of his assessment of anything.

'It was when she mentioned the prowler —'

'Prowler? What, round here?'

'Yes. Someone out of place'd be pretty noticeable, wouldn't they? But I checked the system for any other reports, and asked around, there weren't any.'

'Was she making it up?'

'I don't know. There was something, but I couldn't fathom it. She was very protective of her aunt – if it is her aunt. Specifically asked me not to mention the prowler because she didn't want her worried. She's very frail, walks with a stick.'

Her attention was on negotiating the corner into Palmerston Avenue, halting to let a car out of a driveway. She didn't look forward, to the figure on the opposite pavement.

The opposite pavement.

There she was, miraculously, again. Summoned by Mary's prosaic account, appearing in the full afternoon, a hundred yards away, walking towards them.

His ghost.

His ghost wearing a pleated Indian cotton dress of pale orange, white beads and bangles, white sandals; exactly the clothes any woman would wear in everyday 1990.

His instruction, 'Pull up here,' sounding to his own ears like some deranged adolescent. And even as they stopped, as he took his eyes off her for a moment, she had disappeared again. 'It's all this sodding greenery,' he muttered.

'Um, what, sir?' Mary, confused, her attention on him, could have registered only something on the periphery of her vision.

He said, 'Just, drive slowly – yes. Here.'

White double gates to a gravelled drive, a turn screened by tall conifers; a small white gate to a curving footpath.

If she had a corporeal presence, and now he knew she had, that was where she had gone, along the path, beneath a rose arch, lost immediately from his sight…

No. Not lost. Not now. A shiver of presentiment: anything connecting him with Bankhill shifted him into another dimension.

'That's Fairmead,' Mary said helpfully. 'I went there.'

'Why?'

'It's where she lives, Miss Mannering, the lady who owned the Rover. Was that her? Someone went in just now, didn't they?'

'Did you say Miss Mannering was a spinster of venerable age?'

'Yes.'

'No. Perhaps,' he suggested, 'it was the one who reported the theft.'

'Miss Donovan. It wasn't a theft, sir, or joy-riding, I just know it wasn't.'

'Mary, run through this again.'

She did, with her always conscientious and workaday common-sense.

'OK. They've got the car back, no harm done, there's no point in pursuing this – we haven't time and we're not throwing good money after bad. But what about this prowler?'

'It's a bit vague, she hasn't herself actually seen him.'

'No, but you know we've had a number of reports from – OK out of this area – but you don't need me to tell you that they start off this way with minor offences, stalking, harassment.'

'Sir, the incidents we've had they've always been in working class areas. D'you think...*here?*'

'Why not? He could be widening his base, if he was, there'd certainly be less chance of our linking him up with the previous pattern. You know what happens if he's not caught.'

'Yes. He'll move on to more serious crimes – assault, rape. Get more and more bold.'

'So, maybe it's worth checking up, see if anything else has happened, while we're on the doorstep.'

'Yes,' Mary said uneasily. 'But I promised Miss Donovan – no way would we alarm the old lady. If we go in mob-handed – well, not that you – I mean —'

'Quite right. Tact. If she's on her own, there's no problem. If Miss Mannering's about – kid gloves. I can rely on you. Here's what you say.'

Only the roof of the house was visible from the road. They walked through the barrier of greenery to where a turn revealed it, presenting, with its half-timbering and herringboned brickwork the perfect 1920s Jacobean. They stood beneath a gabled porch with red tiled roof and oak posts, an oak studded front door.

He pulled the bell pull; they waited. Then she opened the door, regarded them both with polite enquiry and, seeing Mary, smiled in recognition, 'Oh, hello.' At once, uncertainty overcame her, she glanced back over her shoulder.

Mary spoke clearly, gaze sweeping beyond her. 'Hallo, Miss Donovan. This is DCI Hunter. We were in the area, just following up in case anyone has come forward with any new information about the car thief...'

Hunter stood speechless. The fine-boned face, fair skin suntanned and scattered with the palest freckles, wide, dark blue, dreaming eyes. Thick, dark blonde hair cut in a completely unfashionable and enchanting bob.

Lowering her voice, Mary said, 'Have you had any other reports about the —'

They both registered the startled look on Daisy's face and, at the same time, in the background, the hovering presence of an immaculately dressed matchstick woman who said, 'How good of you to be so conscientious, won't you come in?'

'I don't think —' Daisy began.

'Thank you,' Hunter said, striding past her.

She watched them being gently ushered into the lounge hall.

What are you doing here? You're supposed to be terrorising the Skinners, not me.

Chapter Fourteen

Sunlight flooded the lounge hall. It was small wonder, when he first saw her he had taken her for a ghost – the setting, the dusk, the clothes – all of a piece with a young woman who had lived in a house like this sixty years ago. And here, uncannily, she appeared again in broad daylight, in reality – no, that was too fragile a concept – with this old woman exquisitely dressed in something panelled in aquamarine lace and silk and was what he had somewhere (God knows how) understood to be a tea gown. This aunt, whoever, had the most sweetly musical voice he had ever heard and looked gently bewildered. He had the impression she frequently did.

They were offered tea, declined, sat down, talked about the Rover, its recovery, in surreal exchanges, Daisy fluffing everywhere. Then Mary was looking across the room at a tall fair-haired man wearing a striped blazer and flannels who had just come in. Hunter wondered where he had left his straw boater and monocle. 'Sorry, Floy, I thought it was —'

'No, they're not here yet. We're expecting guests, you see,' she explained. 'This is my nephew, Clive Mannering. This is the police, Clive, about the Rover.'

'You've not mislaid it again, have you, Daisy? You really are getting careless.' His glance passed innocently over Daisy's narrowed glare before his smile glinted at Mary. He spoke to her in a lowered, confidential voice, 'I hear you're doing splendidly. Keep up the good work. Excuse me.'

While Floy was murmuring, 'I don't drive at present because of my hip operation, Daisy very kindly acts as my chauffeuse, as well as so much else...'

Hunter was asking himself what these people had to do with their lives except dress up and play games and Mary was staring at the door through which Clive had passed, visibly charmed beyond her wits.

Daisy and Floy agreed between themselves that nothing untoward had occurred to them, or their neighbours, since the theft of the car. 'Your chaps got it back again – well, amazingly quickly,' Daisy said.

'Yes. It scarcely had time to go missing, did it?' Hunter agreed.

There was nothing more to be said, he was winging it anyway, if Mary Clegg knew that she would never dare say so. He said to Floy, 'Please don't get up, Miss Donovan can show us out.'

As they passed through the hall an open door gave a glimpse of the dark panelled stately dining room, table set with lace cloth, china, a bowl of roses; the expected visitors.

Daisy shooed them with obvious relief out onto the driveway. Hunter halted deliberately, said, measuredly, 'You made a claim about a prowler.'

'Um... I, um...' She looked unhappy.

'Daisy.' Clive appeared in the porch, signalling, pointing at his watch, smiling apologetically.

Daisy said, 'Heavens, I must get changed, so late. Do excuse me,' and fled into the haven of Fairmead.

Wordless, Hunter strode out to their car. They had only opened the doors when Daisy reappeared. 'Did you drop your – um – Biro.'

She proffered it. So cheap, so anonymous and mass-produced it could have been bought anywhere and belonged to anyone in the British Isles.

Hunter studied it, immovable. Looked at her. 'Something else you've made up, Miss Donovan?'

There was a moment when nothing happened, then, 'Hell, hell, hell,' she said and walked round in a small, wild circle. Fell still and silent.

Hunter said, 'I don't need to tell you wasting police time is an offence.'

'Um, yes. I need to explain.'

Deliberate, he took out his card, handed it to her. 'Yes, I think you do. And I might point out to you, whatever you tell us, we can be discreet.'

'Yes, yes, of course. I'm sorry. I'll – er – yes.'

There was nothing more to say for the moment. They got into their car, snapped into safety belts, pulled away, Hunter with the understanding of how completely Mary Clegg and Brute Force must have been out of their depth with this daft girl.

Mary Clegg said something. He didn't hear, turned, irresistibly glancing back to where Daisy stood, the scented gardens all around, and the sense, in so many becalmed lives, of something helpless, apologetic.

After a silent drive, when they were nearing Talbot Way, Mary said 'Those clothes…they were…dressing up. Do you think they were rehearsing for something?'

He said, 'Rehearsing… That house must have wardrobes of Great Gatsby clothes. She's having us on, Miss Donovan is.'

Exactly what Mary thought, and knew it would make him mad as hell, he couldn't bear to be outwitted. Discreetly overlooking what he had said, but too puzzled to give up, she continued, 'But a lady like Miss Mannering. Why should she want to confuse us?'

'Search me. A woman who's carrying all her mental luggage through a nineteen-thirties twilight, who probably wears hats just like Celia Johnson in *Brief Encounter*, and even speaks like her – *Oh, Elec, this is medness*. How they managed to strangulate A into E, I don't know —'

Mary interrupted, apologetic but firm, 'You're going on a bit, sir.'

'What? Well, she can't be expected to make much sense of 1990, can she? D'you think she knows the British have left India?'

Brick Lane. Hunter had known it all his life, he'd played there, fought there, had fumbling, indiscriminate sex, walked it as a beat bobby; it was a place waiting for something to happen, but nothing ever did. For the past year he had a contact there, of special significance.

Pearl Eugene and her son Dwayne lived in a flat above an electrical repair shop; Pearl was studying for a degree in social sciences, working part-time as a cleaner and caring for Dwayne, crippled by a hit-and-run driver. Big and brave, she had carried him up and down the stairs when there was no one else to do it until Hunter organised the necessary people and money and arranged for a specially adapted chair lift. When he visited he took books and games for Dwayne, magazines for Pearl, something nice for them both – this time a chocolate cake. He took himself, his care, his quiet encouragement, his admiration for their courage and decency.

It was Dwayne's ambition to be a policeman like Mr Hunter; with the dauntlessness of the young, he had no doubt he would bounce back to the vitality that would assure him a career.

From the window of the flat, where he sat in his wheelchair, Dwayne was a conscientious observer of the life in the street. (Hunter often thought life and street a juxtaposition sadly misapplied.) When anything did happen, Dwayne made the most of it, took minutely detailed notes in a thoroughly dispassionate, professional fashion. 'You've told me, Mr Hunter. Observe, record – don't make assumptions or judgements.'

So Hunter, visiting, drew up a chair beside Dwayne, as always, felt the trapped energy in the young body, the quick intelligence, the keen attention. 'Dwayne, you might be able to help me with something —'

'Yes, Mr Hunter?'

'If not, doesn't matter.'

'Oh, go on.'

Hunter laughed. Gave him the date, willed him not to have been applying himself to his homework, whatever.

Dwayne turned back through his notebook, found the day.

Hunter said, 'A car —'

'Yeah —' Dwayne looked up at him with admiration. 'How d'you know? About that car?'

'Tell you later. What have you got there?'

'Everything. Make, colour, registration number. Floy Mannering's Rover. It was a smashing car, Mr Hunter, you never seen anything like that round here. Has it been stolen?'

'It's more a case of lost and found.'

'He must've been bonkers to leave it, just walk away.'

'He?'

'Well… I suppose…it was hard to tell. 'Cos he was tall, but – very skinny, and walking away, not towards me. Long, light-coloured coat, like a mac, and a hat —'

'Hey, Dwayne. Coat? Hat? This hot weather?'

'Yeah. Funny.' He consulted his notes. 'Rotten sort of day, not raining, but grey, as if it was going to. But stuffy. I should have thought —'

'You did think, without realising, and made notes. Shoes?'

'I think some sort of sandals, hard to see 'cos the trouser bottoms were like floppy.'

'Go on.'

'Hat pulled down. A sort of – I dunno, not hats you see about, like bobble hats or baseball caps. Pale colour and like, sort of old-fashioned… A trilby?' he ventured.

'OK. Near enough. Something with a brim that covered his or her hair.'

'Yeah. How d'you know about the car, though, Mr Hunter? Charlie came and took me to the youth centre, when I got back, couple of hours later, it had gone. So I thought he'd just, like come back and driven it away.'

'I don't suppose you've got a time there – when the person left it?'

Dwayne looked crestfallen, shook his head.

'Never mind. What time did you go out with Charlie?'

'What's that got – Oh, I see. It'd be just 'bout quarter to two.'

'It was reported stolen at ten past two.'

'But, that's only about twenty minutes after the geezer left it here.' The puzzled young face cleared, 'Oh, that's why it wasn't here when I got back – your lot had found it. That what you meant? Lost and found. I know – it's the change of shift, isn't it?'

Hunter nodded.

'So. New shift's out on patrol just after two, they're notified of the theft. So many of them come this way to the nick, walking, driving, riding motorbikes, they'd have remembered seeing it here. Yeah. But,' he thought for a moment. 'It sounds daft, as if…nah.'

Hunter looked at him enquiringly.

'Why would someone leave a car like that and then go and report it missing. Don't make sense.'

'Not a bit,' Hunter agreed.

Back at Talbot way, Hunter spoke to Mary Clegg. 'You saw Miss Donovan when she came to report the stolen Rover.'

'With PC Ferris. I wrote out a report.'

'Of course you did. This is something that wouldn't be in it but it is relevant. What was Miss Donovan wearing?'

Mary didn't look surprised, or puzzled, she answered immediately, 'Oh, lovely clothes, made me think of those black and white Thirties films. I got books about them and read about all the designs,' and with all the fashion potential of a gate-legged table, wistfully treated Hunter to a stitch by stitch account of a style long gone, 'a lovely top and sort of floppy trousers, what I think was called cruiser wear…or cruising wear.'

Hunter raised an eyebrow. 'Cruising.'

'It meant something different then.'

'Like a Madam shop?'

'I – er.' A non sequitur? Mary pretended not to notice.

'Was she wearing a coat?'

'Coat, in this weather? No, but, now you mention it, she was carrying one. I think they called them "duster" coats. They covered you up completely, full length, but very light, silky, so when you took them off they sort of folded into nothing and, really, so chic, a sort of straw trilby…'

'Thank you, Mary,' Hunter said, waited, sensing there was more to come.

Intent, without embarrassment or apology, Mary said, 'I thought, when she was speaking to us, that's a troubled young lady. But it was no good saying as much to Brute Force, he just dismissed – oh, sorry —'

'Yes, he dismissed it all as nonsense. If she was in some kind of trouble, it could be family, emotional.'

'If it was, sir, she wouldn't involve the police. She's not the type.'

Type? Miss Daisy Donovan wasn't a type, she was a singularity skimming across his senses; quicksilver encompassing his consciousness…

'…that's why I called round at Fairmead afterwards.'

'Mary, that wasn't necessary. The car had been found, other things need your attention.'

'I know, sir, but I did it in my own time, just – following my nose, and what you said about the prowler, if there'd been anything in it, and we'd ignored it —'

'PC Ferris did.'

'Yes, but er —' What she couldn't tell him was that Brute Force's scepticism, crude as always, not only dismissed the prowler as a figment of Miss Donovan's imagination but went on to observe that those posh tarts had nothing better to do with their time and needed a good seeing to.

'Never mind,' Hunter said, he knew exactly what the expressed view would be of a man who had all the sensitivity of a charging rhino.

'I wanted to see the lie of the land. I thought if I spoke to them together, tactfully, I might get a better idea of the situation.'

'Good. Surest way to do it is to get someone on home ground, especially if they're not expecting you. And did you?'

'No. It was like the other day when we were there. They're so polite, so nice. Miss Donovan was on edge, uneasy – I thought it was because she was afraid I'd put my foot in it, upset Miss Mannering. So I had to draw a blank, told them we'd had no result from our enquiries about who the thief could be, but we were keeping our eyes and ears open. Miss Mannering said it was extremely good of us to be so conscientious and what a jolly worthwhile career it was for a gel —'

Perhaps to compensate for her lack of imagination, Mary had a gift for mimicry that delighted Hunter when he had one day accidentally discovered it. To his fascination, her account – hard information in the form of sublime impersonation – reproduced voices scarcely heard since the high English of the BBC in the 1930s: light open vowels, fluting tones.

Mary, talking more freely, completed the picture of Daisy, obviously making things up, and Floy, without much idea of what was going on at all, in obvious support because she felt it was what the occasion demanded. It must have been a surreal interview.

'I thought then, and when we were there, sir...'

'Go on.'

'I think she was having a bit of fun.'

'So do I,' Hunter said softly, grimly.

Chapter Sixteen

For the second time Daisy walked into Talbot Way divisional headquarters.

The reception area was full of scuffling, shouting activity. She had Hunter's card ready but didn't see how she could get to present it because the desk was unreachable behind two skinny youths, an angry white-haired man and a large woman with a large handbag and an impenetrable Scottish accent – she was doing most of the shouting – who was ricocheting off everyone, including a uniformed policeman.

Daisy, rapidly in retreat, encountered an unnoticed bench along the wall, it struck the back of her legs, making her sit down with a bump. She leapt up again as the melée lurched dangerously close.

An attractive young woman appeared and with no-nonsense expertise elbowed everyone out of the way, steered Daisy clear. 'Can I help? I'm DC Annette Jones – oops.'

Together, they dodged the handbag and an accompanying blast of second-hand Scottish. Daisy said, awe-struck, 'Pissed as a rat at eleven in the morning. That takes some doing.'

'Not round here it doesn't.'

Daisy looked at her respectfully, said, 'I thought police stations are where law and order's kept.'

'We do our best. How can I help?'

Diffident, Daisy showed her Hunter's card. 'I'd like to see…if he's available.'

Available? Six feet two. The strong face, the air of calm containment, dark hair with streaks of grey, eyes like a winter sea. Available. Please.

'I'll find out. If you'd like to come into the interview room. What name shall I say?'

Hunter sat, solid and uncompromising. 'Miss Donovan. This is about the Rover.'

'Yes.'

'And the prowler.'

She looked at him silently before repeating, 'The prowler.'

'Obviously.'

'Why do I feel like a *fait accompli?*'

His fleeting amusement. 'What exactly weren't you telling the truth about?'

She considered this for a moment, then, surprising him, said, 'Mr Hunter, I trained as a dancer.'

'I can see that.' *The swift imprint of your grace on the air around you, the flickering gesture...*

'And I fence.' Inclining forward slightly towards his total incomprehension. 'That means I know how to avoid clumsy feet, and I can defend myself.'

When he'd choked back his laughter he said, 'I really haven't got time for this.'

''Course not. I just wanted to see if you could smile. The Rover.' She hesitated.

He said, 'A 1948 Rover 16 isn't going to stand around indefinitely, unnoticed, on a side street in —'

'Yes. All right. That's what I thought. I admit I left it deliberately and then came and reported it missing. I'm sorry. It was a stupid thing to do.'

'Then why do it?'

'That's the difficult bit.'

'The difficult bit is accounting for why you deliberately wasted police time.'

A hiatus. He could simply sit and drown in the enchantment of her presence. No, he had work to do. But he waited, regarding her and her story, implausible, touching in its vulnerability, a waste of his time, to do with doubtless convoluted family matters. He knew about family by proxy... Divorced, a vengeful wife alienating his daughter, what had he but a theoretical appreciation, a shredded recollection of domestic life. He had a job to do, that was his life. It was as simple as that.

'It's a personal matter,' she said quietly.

'Then why involve us?' It was abrupt, but effective.

'Because I couldn't think of anything else. I had no right to do it. I felt that,' she hesitated, 'at Fairmead we were the subject of unwanted attention. It's a matter I can't discuss with Floy, she would be very upset, so I had this stupid idea that if the police were seen about the place, there would no longer be a problem.'

He registered how carefully she had chosen her words, identifying neither herself nor anyone else.

'Are you being stalked?'

'Good God, no, it's nothing like that.' The astonishment – bewilderment – completely genuine he had no doubt. She was a beautiful young woman, if she was going to make up a credible story she would surely have gone for that, so obvious, simplifying everything, but it had not occurred to her.

He said, 'When you reported the theft of the Rover, you claimed that someone unknown was prowling the neighbourhood. You haven't substantiated this claim and our enquiries have brought nothing to light. You could not only be seriously misleading us but also causing alarm.'

'Oh, no. No, truly, I haven't. I haven't said anything to anyone. I promise, I haven't. I know I said that other people had seen… but I made that up, I'm sorry. I thought if it was just my word you wouldn't believe me.'

'I don't. You haven't given me so far any credible reason for your actions.'

She was suddenly crestfallen, could only repeat, softly, that it was personal and she'd behaved like an idiot, for which she apologised. His momentary reaction was that she was at a loss, doubting what she was doing. Something he could not name communicated itself to him. 'If you have reason to feel threatened, or in any way in danger…there is nothing I can do unless you're honest with me.'

She gave this a moment's thought, stood up, smiled hesitantly, 'Yes, of course. I understand. Thank you for seeing me.' She courteously put out her hand to take his, and in the physical contact there was the sense that only for an instant he had grasped a fleeting presence, insubstantial, desired.

When she returned to Fairmead in the slightly giddied aftermath of the conviction that she might not have achieved anything useful, but she definitely had met the most attractive man ever, it was to find Brenda, coifed and adamant, sitting in the lounge hall with Floy. Energetically voluble, she glanced in Daisy's direction, said in a dismissive voice, 'Haven't you got…something…jobs to do?'

'Absolutely,' Daisy said decisively, sitting next to Floy, registering her tremulousness.

Brenda reverted to a monologue that concerned someone called Annie Preston's girl, who was setting herself up posh.

Something told Daisy that Brenda had not told Floy of her Sunday visit. It wasn't difficult to work out why: Brenda preferred to ignore her existence completely, that meant not talking about her or to her. She wondered how Brenda would react if she said casually that she just come from the police station. If Floy had not been there she would have done.

'— just because she'd got a job as receptionist at the Manor Nursing home. She's only behind a counter, like in a shop, but looking down her nose at everyone. Thinks she can get away with telling people who they can and can't see.'

Floy had nothing to say, she gazed out to the garden, her thin fingers pleating and smoothing her lace handkerchief. Brenda fidgeted, glaring about in inexplicable anger, making small huffing noises. A density of misunderstandings, unspoken intent, bluster and doubt thickened the air.

Daisy said, 'It could be the policy there,' with a thought for the bossy receptionist. Perhaps there were several, specially trained.

'Policy, whose *policy*?' Brenda jeered.

Floy winced, murmured, 'Possibly the management, the medical —'

Brenda, fishing paper tissues from her handbag, unaware of irony, muttered about what sort of policy was it to be rude to people. Daisy wondered why on earth she should be concerned with the working arrangements at the Manor, felt an inner sinking: she hadn't managed to warn the Skinners off, after all. They had probably been regrouping for a second strike.

Perhaps as a result of being ignored, Brenda became strident, 'Well, who is *she*, I'd like to know, to tell my Mam and Dad who

they can and can't see? *I'd* say folks well off enough to pay those
sort of prices can decide for theirselves, thank you very much.
But, oh no, Miss Posh takes it on herself to order them about, she
should have more respect for older people who's as good if not
better nor her. *Have to see Sister*, indeed. And what's it got to do
with *her* —'

Daisy had a mind trip: was this what Sister had hinted? So few
of his old friends left...visitors presenting themselves...I exercise
my own judgement. She waited for Brenda to draw breath, asked
smoothly, 'Why did your parents go to visit Mr Stephenson?'

Brenda instantly turned her head away, made a thrusting
movement with her arm as if sweeping Daisy out of sight, and
began to tell Floy about the new dishwasher our John had
acquired.

Daisy sat staring at her, coldly recalling the kitchen at Canal
Street. Big John. That grim old couple. Her sense of their silent
rage – it was as if they had distilled it and transferred it to Brenda
to carry here and spread around Floy.

Daisy's mind shouted *caution*; but she would not be put down,
she said distinctly in an interested voice, 'We had no idea your
grandparents knew Hugh.'

On the stately Knole sofa, Brenda's body braced in outrage, she
said to Floy, 'My parents have an old friend, a very old friend
staying there. They had the decency to call in on him, her, bring
a bit of comfort...'

'How awfully kind,' Daisy said. 'But do you mean they weren't
allowed to visit this – er – old friend? That really sounds
draconian, I'm sure Sister Wainwright wouldn't —'

Brenda had managed to manoeuvre into a position where she
could abruptly and deliberately turn her back on Daisy. She
leaned urgently towards Floy. 'This is between us, as family.
You've not been to see him, so you don't know what they'll be
getting up to there.'

To Daisy it was all becoming more improbable by the minute:
an 'old friend' (whose gender seemed to be a mystery to Brenda)
of the grandparents in that wildly expensive place? Perhaps he –
she – had won the lottery. All right, concede that. What could the

grandparents possibly have to do with Hugh? But, what had Sister been trying to say…? And Brenda, refusing to answer her question, had the twitchiness of a woman making up ground after a slip.

If I ask her again, if she speaks to me, it won't be the truth, and I'll get angry and an unforgivable row will blow up.

She coughed deliberately, leaned forward, had the satisfaction of Brenda darting a venomous glance, before continuing to hector Floy, a vermilion fingernail tapping on the chair arm for emphasis, '— odds are he wouldn't even know you, so you don't want to be going there —' It had obviously not occurred to her that Daisy could have seen Hugh.

Floy said nothing at all, she had gathered herself into a ramrod attitude, monumentally waiting for Brenda to leave.

Daisy knew when to wait for the calm reaches of the day to speak to Floy, although it seemed impossibly long before the rhythm of Fairmead re-established itself. A casual reference to Brenda, the query, what had she come for? resulted only in Floy turning away into her private consolations, without words, shaking her head.

In bed the sleep eluding conviction that Floy was deliberately keeping something from her. Because she didn't trust her? Because she thought her too stupid to understand? For comfort, she sought the last time there was humour in Brenda's awful presence: the afternoon tea, when she had marched in as the Prendergasts left, 'Grendell's mother'. She thought about this minutely, everything that happened. Brenda trying to eavesdrop on Floy. Our John making himself at home in the kitchen. Floy coming in, pleased with the news of Quill's visit. She wondered if she was imagining it, or had nothing really been the same since then?

Chapter Seventeen

Floy had entertained friends to a buffet lunch, Daisy, helping to clear away, looked out of the dining room window.

'Who's that?'

A short, plump young woman in T-shirt and leggings she should never have even considered, and two small children, one tramping on each side, rounded the evergreens.

Floy said breathlessly, 'I think it must be one of the...um...one of Brenda's...'

For Daisy there was a feeling of something aghast: why am I always looking out of the window and seeing bloody Skinners invading Fairmead?

Floy went on, 'Darling, I can't possibly, I don't...'

'No, no, don't worry, I'll head them off.'

But by the time she got to the front door and opened it, they had vanished. She heard voices from the side path – they had obviously gone round to the kitchen, our John's habitual way. Her choice was ignominious pursuit – No. Instead, sprinting through the house, she was out of the kitchen door and meeting them as they rounded the side of the garden storeroom.

It was Edna. Enid? Yes, our John's exemplary wife. She did not look directly at Daisy, her whole manner was evasive – shyness or slyness? Her voice was loud, badly pitched. 'It's ages since Auntie Florrie saw her grandchildren.'

Grandchildren... Before the staggering inexactitude Daisy was speechless. The Skinners had the most garbled way of hi-jacking relationships. Her instinct was to refute, clear the matter up before it bedded itself into fraudulent enrolment, then she read in Enid a bovine acceptance of anything life dealt out: she would always do as she was told because other people were always in authority, positive about what they were doing in ways that were beyond her. Which left Daisy wondering – as she was plainly incapable of acting on her own behalf, who had told her to come and see Floy, and why?

'It was nice of you to bring —' she frantically sought names '— er to see Floy. Please excuse her, she's not at all well.'

The boy and girl, like their mother short and overweight, dressed in showily inappropriate sportswear, regarded Daisy with the occluded look of children who were warned, constantly, against strangers – and somewhere, as they glanced around, the sense of denied adventure. She thought of all the denials of her own childhood, went and took their small, pliant hands. 'Tell you what, come into the garden for a while.' She led them forward, explaining, 'There used to be a swing, jolly nice. It's gone now, but we climbed that tree there. Shall we gave a go at it now?'

'They don't climb —' their mother began but the children were already on their way.

It was a friendly sycamore, misshapen with age and years of loppings; Daisy climbed with them, swung and scrambled, their laughter and shouts rang through the garden. Enid stood close, shaking her head in disbelief at Daisy, murmuring, 'Well, I never,' more often calling to Shirley and Lance to be careful. Their disregard made it plain they were told so often to be careful they no longer heard her. 'They're OK,' Daisy said, making sure they were as they pulled and pushed her and she helped them scramble.

She judged when they had had enough and might get over-excited, shooed them all into the summer house. 'Now, what about lemonade and ice cream?' As she went to the house she was pursued by an almost agonised, 'Be careful, Shirley,' and turned to find herself sedately accompanied by the small girl who yelled back in pained self defence, 'I'm *helping*'.

In the summer house, Enid fussed over not making a mess, Daisy said honestly, it really didn't matter here, it was more or less the garden. She had never before had occasion to wonder if there was a limit on the variations of not spilling anything and not ruining things. There was, she discovered, when Enid set out, with added stridence, to repeat them all; stupefied by boredom she could almost imagine Enid said something like, 'And when's Quillie coming to visit Him as is in the Nursing Home?'

When she realised 'Him as is in the Nursing Home' could only mean Hugh Stephenson, she asked, bewildered, 'You *know* Hugh?'

'It's John's mum's mam and dad,' Enid said, energetically untying and retying the laces of Lance's trainers.

The grandparents' notional friend at the Manor occurred to Daisy, but she asked, 'What is?'

'Is he, then?' Enid began on Tracey's laces.

'I don't know what you're talking about,' Daisy said wildly.

Enid, who had not looked at Daisy since they'd come into the summer house, launched into energetic scolding about the 'the *state* of those clothes, the mess made by all that climbing about.'

Daisy glanced down at her Bermuda shorts and cotton shirt and said well, yes, her own were in the same state but the washing machine would soon sort them out, then asked carefully, 'Why are you interested in Quill seeing Hugh? Has somebody told you to ask?'

'Oh, him,' Enid said, with a noise that sounded like a laugh, then, 'Look at the time, you two, come on —'

Daisy knew she would get nowhere. Enid had been used, with probably no idea why. By whom? None of that family were capable of subtlety. Except Edward.

She saw them off, walked them to the gate, the boy said, 'Can we come back soon and play?'

'Now, listen,' she squatted down to their level, put her arms round them. 'Miss Mannering isn't well at the moment, she needs it to be very quiet. You understand?'

The boy said, 'Not well. Like old Mr Jones —'

Oh, Jesus, I've had more than enough of your old Mr Jones, poor sod.

'Not at all,' she said, interrupting a disturbingly exact repetition of our John's imitation of Mr Jones's damaged speech (perhaps it was a kind of family entertainment, like singing round the piano). 'She's had an operation on her hip and she needs to rest and get her strength back. But when she's feeling better, then we'll see.' A serious nod from the boy, a soft, damp kiss from the girl. Enid, angry about something, snatched their hands, '*Come on.*'

Daisy watched them walk away. When they reached the corner the children turned and waved, smiling. Enid plodded on.

Floy, with a headache, obviously did not wish to have any account of what had occurred. 'Tomorrow, darling.'

Yes.

At six thirty, Daisy answered the door. She was going dancing with her friend Stephanie, Floy was not expecting visitors, she had planned an evening of music and reading. The caller was a small man – to Daisy's five foot eight – shifting on the porch with a hunched aggression; he wore a baseball cap tilted so far forward his brow and eyes were invisible. He began to shout, a small hoarse shout. She took a step back.

She had ill treated his son's kids.

What?

Put them in danger. A strong waft of beer. Frightened them. Making them climb fucking trees.

One tree. The darling old sycamore. Their joy in the freedom. 'Who are you?' She didn't need to ask, although she had no recollection of seeing him on the Sunday lunchtime she had called at the Skinners'. Mr Hutton, Brenda's husband. She found herself, wrenched from normality, taking on this bird-boned man who hid his eyes and was fuelled by beer and a personal rage.

'Your daughter-in-law, Enid —' it was difficult to speak firmly with her heart lurching, with this verbal assault and everything familiar in the quiet of the evening destroyed. Don't let Floy hear. She explained carefully how Enid had called bringing Shirley and Lance, the ice cream and lemonade.

From the region beneath the visor of the baseball cap his mouth moved. 'No way to treat people as come calling proper. You're going to finish up in a cortalore, I'll see to that. A fucking cortalore.'

'How can I speak to you if I can't see you? Will you take that cap off.'

He said something that sounded like *whaa?* Then, 'I know you and your sort, fucking cheats. You wait. Our Edward won't let that ponce in Ireland get away with nuffin. He'll show you.'

What he shouted next she could not bother to work out as she needed her effort to get rid of him. Heart pounding, she pushed him back (loathing the excited touch of body through his shirt) towards the screen of evergreens. She had managed, distractedly, to translate the often repeated, bewildering word as 'court of law'. All this, all the while, to a wild counterpoint, the revving of motorcycles. As he scuttled from sight, there was a diminution of sound, engines idling, then voices, shouts… Like the ones she had heard when she walked away down the road from the Skinners with Big John.

She went back indoors, shut herself into the downstairs loo to take deep breaths, run cold water over her wrists, sure way to cool down. Calmer, she thought what she must immediately do, went into the hall and made a phone call. *Hey, so sorry, can't manage tonight, awful migraine…*

In the garden room, Floy said, 'Darling, there were sort of noises from motorbikes or something when you went to answer the door. Who was it?'

'Oh, the bikes were just going past – it was one of those double glazing outfits.'

'I really don't know why they bother. Stephanie should be picking you up soon, shouldn't you be getting changed? You don't want to be late.'

'No, no, er – I just checked with Steph and she can't make it this evening, so I thought I'd give it a miss.'

Floy murmured disappointment on her behalf, unsuccessfully concealing the pleasure that she would have Daisy's company.

After that, how can I possibly leave her alone?

I'm telling lies, I'm misrepresenting facts, I'm getting afraid to open the door…

What am I going to do?

She couldn't take the Skinners on on her own, that was for sure.

Chapter Eighteen

In bed, churningly awake, she collected and examined so many disparate elements: the Skinners' suspected criminality – perhaps all in her mind; the victimisation of their visits – how dare they? What did Floy's gentle days have to do with them? Their obsession with Hugh Stephenson and Quill extending, bizarrely, to the bovine Enid; and God knew what she had said to her father-in-law.

And then, the abrupt tilt of connection: the Skinners and Edward. The filtering of a most reluctant memory...

Two years ago, when she stayed with Quill. The glimmer of the winter night through the long windows of the library – the room that spoke so much of Quill: the amiable company of his books; cracked, age-darkened portraits of loved horses and dogs; the faded tapestry of Saint Patrick banishing the snakes from Ireland.

Edward said, 'Quill tells me you're leaving. How... unexpected.' He trailed the word provocatively.

No, her departure wasn't unexpected, not to him.

He hadn't planned it – how could he? It had been her impulse to take Quill's golden retriever Barnaby for his evening walk to the ruined church by the river. The air was silky, full of tiny flitting bats; a heron rose, a great, lazily flapping creature, sweeping silver overhead, powerful, exquisite. And then the high stone wall enclosing the silence of neglect, the iron gate eaten away by rust and age, opening to waist-high grass, the lonely tower held together by massed ivy; headstones tilting and crumbling. Barnaby dashing off, slinking back. 'Come on you daft dog, there's nothing to be afraid of.' Setting an example, striding along the only path, turning a corner of the dense yew hedge.

And there, in a bower.

The density of foliage had baffled sound, the grunts, the gasps of two men rutting. Edward, lips drawn back in a ferocious smile, staring directly at her. Her obscured view of the other man, fleetingly no more than a down-turned, curly dark head – how could she want to know what friend, neighbour of dear Quill was buggering his lover? It was their private business entirely – but Edward, forewarned by Barnaby, had heard her voice, had known that path would lead her there. This she understood later. In the tumbling confusion of the moment she turned, blundering away, her gaze fetching up on a collapsed vault, its open door, a litter of bones of the long, long dead. A chill caught her, a shiver of premonition.

To Quill she made some excuse about leaving the next day. 'Oh, darling, must you?' He didn't attempt to dissuade her, his regret was as genuine as the sad knowledge on his face.

And then she was alone with Edward in the library, after dinner, scaldingly aware she had no idea how to talk to him. Would he pretend nothing had happened, would he excuse it as the overwhelming passion of the moment, would he explain it in some other (for God's sake what) terms?

He lounged, well fed, well wined, (Daisy had been scarcely able to eat a mouthful) a pampered boy-man, golden-haired, who knew himself – at the times when he could choose his setting, his circumstance – treacherously attractive.

She looked steadfastly away, out of the window, towards the glow-worm night.

'Don't go, Daisy,' he said softly, teasing. 'I'm surprisingly versatile. We could —'

'Oh God, what a bloody cheap line.'

'It turned you on, in the churchyard. Don't tell me it didn't.' He allowed his feral allure to show, and his vicious satisfaction in it. No pretence, no denial. She had seen, would never speak of it to Quill, to anyone; her presence, her knowledge, engaged her in the act. He was expert at that.

'Turned me on, what are you talking about, you whore? And as for coming on to me – I'd rather clean out drains.'

'Who are you calling a whore? Poor little Daisy, you are so like me —'

'*What?*'

'Hasn't it occurred to you? Both of us, we don't belong

anywhere. And because of that, you've always clung round the edges of the oh-so-secure Mannerings. Yes, look at it, Daisy. Nobody wanted you. Not even your mother, certainly not your mother. Mine died, yours has just never cared.'

'I don't sell myself.'

'Of course you do, you pathetic little cow. You sell yourself to the Mannerings —'

'No, I don't. I care about them, they're – I'd do anything for them. They *matter* to me. But you, you want to come between Quill and his family, his friends.'

His mild surprise that she should make such an accusation. 'I already have. *Family* – what is it? They mean fuck all to me. My family, I wouldn't piss on them if they were on fire.' A look of malign triumph. 'Still, they've had you sussed ever since we were kids. Skinny tart with your face pressed against the window of the big house. Always trailing after Clive and me – you in your clothes too big because they were cast-offs from the Mannerings' posh friends —'

She was silenced by a vividly painful reversal of time. The boys six years older, more observant, knowing, secure in their own world; and Edward always so well-dressed. The day he called for Clive at Fairmead, bringing with him two shabby boys in dirty grey flannels, soiled shirts and scuffed shoes. They barged about the kitchen, laughing loudly, talking in coarse shouts, making farting noises.

Aghast, frightened, she retreated to the side larder, slipping into its cool, concrete-ledged space. With the door secretly ajar, she glimpsed Floy – colour on her cheekbones – standing stiff backed, contained. 'You must leave, this isn't a playground.'

Edward briefly in view, unbelievably smirking. He was then, what? Thirteen. Tall for his age. His eyes on a level with Floy's, his voice insolent. 'These are my cousins, miss. Reenie said —'

'My sister Irene is no longer here to say anything. You have heard me, now go. Clive, a moment.'

Half-heard words, her attention spinning from Floy and Clive then through the tiny, wire-meshed window where the boys were outside, making gestures towards the kitchen that she knew were in every sense of the word rude, although she could not have specified where 'rude' was impolite or shockingly and unknowably *rude*. When Clive went slinking out to join them, she tiptoed into the empty kitchen. Floy was crossing the hall, making for the telephone alcove. 'Aunt Floy —'

'Not now, Daisy, there's a good girl.'

She had never heard that sharp tone in Floy's voice, never before or since felt the trembling of scarcely controlled, distressed anger. She crept up to the games room, which at that time was her room, grabbed Pooh and Piglet and sat rocking them in her arms.

Was it that day Quill came? Betrayingly, he had no time for her, 'Darling, not now.' A door closing, quenching voices, 'Quill, you must put your foot down. I will not have that boy —'

That winter evening in Quill's house was the last time she saw Edward, their childhood catching them up, unfurling around them. Whatever poison he poured over her, she maintained her inviolable defence: They are people I love. You don't know the honour in that.

What was there to understand about Edward's hold over Quill? Sexual, emotional, yes, that was forgivably human, but she had never grasped how it extended to the unlikely, unwanted family ties, so persistently kept up by the Skinners with Floy. How many people beyond herself, Floy, Clive, knew Edward was not capable of honestly earning his own living, needing Quill as protector, paying his debts, giving him a lifestyle he felt he deserved but could never afford. Did any of the Skinners? How often Quill had bailed him out from financial deals of stupefying complexity that somehow, forever foundered – never through any fault of his own – when he was operating in the money mania of the Eighties, cheek by jowl with the yuppies and asset strippers, corporate raiders. All aggressive words so suited to Edward's predatory and devious nature.

What she took away, unwillingly, from her curtailed visit – tension, raised voices behind the doors of another room, undercurrents – became explicable later. Quill telephoned and with a brave melancholy told her that Edward had left. 'A civilised enough arrangement, Daisy, but he needed to go his own way.'

Her relieved, selfish rejoicing, *you're free of him*. But then, what was Quill suffering? How betrayed, lonely. 'Quill, would you like me to come and – keep you company for a while?'

It was spring by then, the countryside all around him bursting with promise and green shoots, the dawn air sweet, the rain silver and swift as mercy. 'No, darling. *I* will take you to Italy.'

When three days had gone by and he had said nothing of Edward, she offered, delicately, her willingness to listen if he cared to talk. With equal delicacy he declined, in his diffidence she read his need, kept quiet; you didn't do anything with such knowledge, you just held it in trust.

So she never mentioned the separation to anyone, not even Floy, and when, months later, she heard through friends that Edward was back with Quill, 'visiting', she was, equivocally, almost glad.

Chapter Nineteen

The next morning the euphoria of the morning run through quiet roads and interlacing footpaths was jeopardised by the marching figure of Mrs Bulstrode. The sight of her was enough for Daisy's inadequate history lessons to surface with reference to the second world war: the massive lumps of concrete on the beaches of England, immovable and ugly tank traps. Mrs Bulstrode was a tank trap.

She lived almost opposite Fairmead in a house that, amidst surrounding leafiness, was stripped down to gravel, paving and concrete. Its uncurtained windows (Mrs Bulstrode believed only blinds were hygienically dust free) had a stark vigilance, pitilessly searching out local comings and goings.

A forceful woman whose husband had left her, to no one's surprise, she was chair of several committees which to Daisy meant wherever she could park her large bottom. She was on her daily walk with her Bedlington terrier, an inoffensive creature called Stamford. In Daisy's world, no dog should be called Stamford.

Approaching, Mrs Bulstrode was in full throat. Stamford had been distressed, very much distressed the previous evening by the noise of motorcycles.

'Oh, darling, I'm so sorry.' Daisy crouched and whispered into its woolly ear. 'I can tell you, sodding awful things happen in the lives of us human beans.'

'And, Daisy, this man who called on you —'

'Double glazing salesman.'

'— and when he came out, one of these motorcycle persons gave him a helmet and he got on the back of this – conveyance – and they all roared off. Very peculiar, evidently they – whosoever – were waiting for him – to considerable noise and disruption. In this neighbourhood we're just not used to that kind of thing. What firm?'

'What?'

'This double glazing company. They can be made to account for the conduct of their employees. What firm did he represent?'

Useless to protest that she had no idea, she hadn't been interested enough to ask, who listened to what anyone said when they came to the door?

Mrs Bulstrode did, most carefully, and made a note in case there should be repercussions. And as in this case there were, Daisy must ask around to find out who else he had called on. Then complain to his firm, nip this sort of thing in the bud. 'After all, Daisy, we had the police all over here not long ago, and that was something to do with you.'

'Not me personally.' Daisy took savage pleasure in the outright lie. 'The Rover was stolen, I can scarcely be held responsible for that.' But she was, giddyingly, from the best of intentions.

'I concede that. But the police should know there's man knocking on doors and not accounting for himself. If you don't inform them, I shall.'

Why? They already know what a prune I can make of myself, they don't need your help. Oh, shut up Mrs Bulstrode, go and savage someone else.

She stroked Stamford. His look of permanent apology conveyed he knew his mistress drove everyone mad, but she cared most sweetly for him. What more could a dog ask?

Daisy said things briskly in a tone that sounded like agreement with all Mrs Bulstrode's strictures, asked just, please, don't talk to Floy about this, it would upset her very much, unnecessarily.

A severe look. 'I do know how to behave, Daisy. Grace Wilmot is due back from South Africa soon, is she not?'

'Don't know.' It was a kind of genteel mugging – any more trouble and Mrs Bulstrode would enlist Grace's help in subduing it and that would mean Floy, as next door neighbour, inevitably involved.

In the hall, Daisy took up the morning's post. Amongst her distracted sorting she came upon another crumpled, scrawled envelope. After her run-in with Mrs Bulstrode, she was too bludgeoned to pay attention to it. The routine of the breakfast tray went some way towards calming her, although Floy asked if she was all right.

'Oh, Mrs Bloody Bulstrode, complaining about the noise of those motorbikes yesterday.'

'To you. Why on earth should she? Do you think she was born with that voice? Have you noticed it's perfectly pitched for opening meetings and calling committees to order. Or perhaps she practised. Oh, Daisy, this is from Grace, she'll be coming home on the seventeenth.'

'Super.' Mrs Bulstrode would have pounced on another victim by then.

But when Daisy went up for her tray, it was as if the playfulness and ease had never happened. Floy, strained and pale, said she had started a headache, would stay in bed, no phone calls or visitors. Daisy translated – only bone fide visitors – she was resigned to becoming as vigilant as Sister Wainwright.

On the way downstairs she wondered if something in the post had upset Floy. Surely, she would have said, talked it over – Daisy paused, looking back at the closed bedroom door. One of those scruffy envelops had been in the post, she'd overlooked it... Was it the same as the other one? She couldn't be sure. She could scarcely go back and look. Anyway, there had been no sign of any post when she collected the tray. Floy had tidied it all away.

She let her coffee grow cold, despising herself for her feeble yearning to shift her helplessness on to someone else. Or at least talk, and share it. Clive was away at a book fair for at least a week, even if he had been here he would refuse to involve himself.

What she could not do was talk to Floy's friends, with whom she had only superficial contact, it would be unforgivable, cause enormous embarrassment, to go about gossiping amongst them. In their reticence and politeness they were assorted versions of Floy. If she could talk to someone robust, uninvolved – like the efficient PC Mary Clegg. Or the equally efficient DC Jones – Daisy's envious recollection of how summarily she had dealt with the confusion at Talbot Way, steered her clear...

Women the same age as Daisy, but so capable they could only highlight her own incompetence. Although she could scarcely have been expected to know – until PC Clegg explained to her –

that the Rover was found so quickly not just because it was noticeable but also because of a shift change. She had a mad vision of Mrs Bulstrode frog-marching her into the police station to parade once again her inability to get anything right.

She thought about that shift change. For some time.

Looked at her watch.

Loitering outside sub divisional headquarters on the edge of the police parking area, she could scarcely have felt more conspicuous or more furtive. All in the hope of seeing a friendly face. Not the testosterone charged Constable Ferris, no. Not – she daren't even imagine how he would react – DCI Hunter.

Rain had threatened all day, occurred offstage to the accompaniment of thundercloud rumblings, the air stifled with the threat of a downpour – she could scarcely hang about in that.

Then there was DC Jones, making her way through the parked cars. Daisy didn't wait, made a rapid approach, smiling in fake surprise, 'Gosh. Hallo. Daisy Donovan, you probably won't remember.'

DC Jones halted, studied her. 'Why do I have the feeling I've just been bushwhacked?'

A martyred, I-never-get-away-with-anything expression. 'Is it so obvious?'

'Obvious. You're rotten at this. Don't ever take up crime. What are you doing hanging around here?'

'Well, I remembered what PC Clegg said, when they recovered the Rover, about the shift change…and I thought, if I waited around, I might catch one of you.'

Annette politely pointed out that she was CID and it didn't apply.

'Oh, doesn't it? No, I see. Sorry, but this isn't official.'

'Never mind, you just struck lucky, you got me. And?'

'Well, I'd rather like some help, some advice, I mean. Oh, I'm keeping you from —' as Annette glanced at her watch.

'No, it's all right. Date later. I've got time.' The first great spreading splotches of rain splattered around them. 'Let's sit in my car.' What she did not say was that she'd had an account of something so uncharacteristically garbled from Mary Clegg she could not help but be intrigued…

The stormlight turned pewter, rain drummed on the roof of the car. Daisy sat silent; Annette opted for the stringent approach. 'If you're in some kind of trouble, Miss Donovan —'

'Daisy.'

'OK. Annette. Are you?'

'Not me, not personally. There are some people who are – associated with Miss Mannering —'

'Associated?'

'A rather distant connection by marriage. They're a bit rough and can be rude…'

Annette listened in silence, put together the stumbling narrative of people who kept calling on Miss Mannering and distressing her with their unwelcome presence, registered Daisy's paranoid insistence that they weren't family, although they appeared to have married into it, at some past time.

And Daisy, hearing her own words spilling out, halted on images of Big John, Emma, little Bert. 'Of course, some of them are perfectly nice, I don't mean all the Skinners are dreadful.'

The ones we know are, Annette could have said. Every town, every district, every area, had its small time villains whose surname was enough to brand blameless individuals, but as far as Chatfield was concerned, the Skinners deserved everything they got. For shop lifting, drunk and disorderly, minor criminal damage; they were fined or sentenced at the magistrates court so regularly Annette was surprised Daisy hadn't come across them in one of their many appearances in the local paper – but then she was a visitor, not a resident, she wouldn't be interested in neighbourhood minutiae. Miss Mannering was, though, must know of their reputation – and so presumably had kept it from Daisy.

Sorting through a mental file of names, addresses, incidents, she thought it possible, but could not be sure, that the Skinners of the Easton estate were not known to CID or uniform. If they were a comparatively respectable bunch, this made the unlikeliness of their connection to the rarefied Mannerings just about credible. But still, a woman of Miss Mannering's fastidiousness would never wish to talk to *anyone* about them.

'Daisy, this is pretty low-level stuff. In fact, it's scarcely visible.'

'No, I know. Feeble, isn't it?'

'What I mean is, these are personal matters, not our concern. If there was an obvious threat, or intimidation, and Miss Mannering made an official complaint —'

'No, I'm sure she'd never do that,' Daisy said, confirming Annette's assessment.

'You could do it on her behalf, you know.'

Daisy looked shocked. 'Oh, no, not without speaking to her first, she's such a very private person, she couldn't bear to have her personal life...'

'Listen, the best thing for you is to keep your distance from the Skinners. I'm sure you're capable of handling them – if you have to – otherwise, just keep your distance.'

Daisy gave her a measuring look. 'Are you saying something...off the record?'

Amongst the first, hard learnt lessons – *anything you say off the record can come back and bite you.* 'No, I'm not. But if people are found guilty of misdemeanours, offences, that'd be a matter of public record. But – so what? You wouldn't choose to mix with them, would you? No. So, as I said, keep your distance.'

After a pause, Daisy said, 'I'm going to think about that.'

The storm had fled, leaving hugely cleansed, breathable air. Annette offered, 'Can I give you a lift somewhere? You're not in the famous Rover are you?'

'No. Is it? Famous?'

'Notorious. All round the nick.'

'Oh, God. No, thanks.' Daisy explained she was staying on in town, going dancing.

'Hey, ballroom, I've always wished I could do that.'

'Come September, I'll teach you.' She told Annette about her plans, her partnership with Ellie.

'A dancing school. Yes, please. Somehow, I wouldn't have thought – well, ballet, maybe, but —'

'Because I don't wear sequins and have my hair done by a structural engineer.'

Annette slid down in her seat, breathed, 'Sorry, sorry. Was that awful of me?'

'No, I'm used to it. I'll still teach you. You don't think...'

'What?'

'Er...does your boss have a burning desire to learn the tango?'

Annette gave thought to everything she knew about Hunter. 'Tell you what, Daisy, I think he might already know.'

Hunter, opening his office window after the downpour, looked out on rushing gutters, sparkling, spreading puddles, and Daisy getting out of Annette's car. He watched her walk away; Annette drive off in the other direction. The next day he asked Annette, 'Did I see you with Miss Donovan yesterday?'

She told him about the Skinner connection and how some of them had previous.

'Can any of this be linked to the notional prowler at Bankhill?'

She looked at him blankly. 'The what?'

'She didn't mention him? No. I wonder why not. Maybe she's trying to cut down on the number of people here who don't believe her.'

After a silence in which Annette thought all manner of things, she asked, 'What shall I do, guv?'

When Daisy came back from her morning run, Mrs Lowe had a message for her. It was understood between them that Floy, for the present, was not answering the phone. Messages were passed, filtered, filleted, censored, anything, depending on Daisy or Mrs Lowe's discretion. 'A Miss or Mrs Annette Jones.'

'Oh, yes.'

'Can you meet her for a drink at the Blue Piano on Spencer Street, perhaps supper later.'

'Great. Thank you, Mrs Lowe.'

Just before seven, in the painstakingly restored Art Deco of the Blue Piano, which happened to be one of Clive's watering holes – its elegance, he claimed, almost matched his own – Daisy bought a glass of wine, selected the *Telegraph* from the available newspapers, and sat down in a corner. After a few moments she was aware of the unmistakable bulk of a male presence taking the chair across from her. What to do? Read on? Glare? She settled for rattling the newspaper, then looked up.

'Hallo,' Hunter said.

Chapter Twenty

He never understood it at the time, a charged and golden traverse from one line of ascent to another. Hesitant words over the telephone, shared laughter, her scent, one body imprinted on the other by a touch, a kiss…no more. She said, 'Um, do you mind if we wait?' He said he would wait forever. Provided that was soon.

When she had sat, cornered, in the Blue Piano, rattling her newspaper and then gathering her dignity to confront the unwelcome male presence… The start of recognition, glinting enjoyment. She asked delicately, 'Is this official?'

'No, it's personal.' But he never understood then, he never understood how personal beyond a lifetime's comprehension.

They went walking in Cheshire, she took him through coverts, down bridleways where she had ridden and hunted with Floy and Quill. He showed her where he had picked bluebells, carried them triumphantly home on his second-hand bicycle to his mother.

She was in town buying shoes, they arranged to meet for lunch. She chose the rendezvous: a car park on one of the roads to Bankhill that passed through the outskirts of Chatfield, whizzed up in a smart H reg Mini Cooper. 'Did you decide on this instead of shoes?'

Her sparkling smile. 'It belongs to my friend Stephanie, she's in Australia for six weeks, she's lent it to me.'

With her he had stopped guarding his feelings, his face said everything about the disappointment of not getting his hands on the Rover.

'I *think* I've just taken a toy away from a small boy. Have a play with this.'

'Daisy, I can't even get in it.'

'Well, you can have a go at the Rover soon, promise. Floy won't mind. Consolation prize for now, I'll take you somewhere special for a drink before lunch. Come on.'

They walked through the sunlight and dusty shadows of a residential backwater. There were a few shops here and there, family businesses lingering into the age of the supermarket, and he had heard of a herbalist but had never been there. Daisy knew where to find it, down a carriageway between the long back gardens of Edwardian houses to an odd shaped area with a patch of green and a massive chestnut tree.

Small, golden scrolled lettering: Deary Brothers. They were tall, thin, wore long white coats, their narrow faces knew hermetic secrets, they moved soundlessly about a shop that smelt of cloves and peppermint with a marble counter and mahogany shelves of jars and carboys full of coloured liquids. An engraved glass partition guarded a space of polished tripod tables with wrought iron legs, comfortably padded settles against the walls. They sat in the dimly filtered light; Hunter gazed at their tall, fluted glasses of hot sarsaparilla. 'I'm in a time warp, aren't I?'

'Well, it's been in the same family since 1898. They don't believe in rushing anything.'

'Thank God. If this was a pub,' Hunter said, 'it'd be a —'

'I know, Frog and Nightgown.'

In all his personal relationships he knew about the value of private compulsions, of leaving room for the slow release of confidences. Nevertheless, she had entered into his orbit in his professional capacity, and, admitting to himself he was half dazed by his feelings for her, he needed to face reality. An intelligent woman had done some impressively unaccountable things, her previous explanations for them were inadequate, he set himself to discover why. His questioning of her was so skilful she scarcely realised what was happening until she had revealed all kinds of matters, mostly inconsequential or speculative.

He considered only briefly the 'theft' of the Rover. That surreal episode had entered into the mythology of Talbot Way so immovably he could only feel that the least harm to anyone was just to leave it there.

The prowler. She had admitted this was an invention, but no matter how carefully he questioned her he could not bring its relevance to the surface of her mind; it was only too plain to him that she had externalised what she saw as a threat, not to herself, but to Floy.

And the threat itself? The unwanted, obtrusive Skinners. This was social not criminal – and how they had ever in the first place crossed the threshold of Fairmead he couldn't imagine. When Daisy explained about Irene and Stanley's marriage, it began to make sense. She conveyed to him, at several removes, how touching the mature union, its joy and fulfilment. But, in her knowledge, only Stanley and his son ever visited Floy during the short marriage and were generously welcomed, and continued to be after Irene's death. But then Stanley died only months later, and it seemed it was after that the Skinners began to turn up, the link being their direct relationship to Edward.

'Do you mean he moved in there?'

'God, no. Floy couldn't put up with him, he was, well, troublesome. Occasionally he stayed with Clive because they were friends, but Clive's parents didn't encourage him. His family sort of passed him about amongst themselves for a few years, then when I suppose he was old enough he just – took off. They're sort of his legacy,' she paused, with the look of a prompted thought. 'I don't know where I got the impression somewhere that they expected Edward to inherit something from Irene, I think Floy might have paid his school fees – but I couldn't possibly talk to her about money.'

'So vulgar,' he said, gently teasing.

But she said, 'Mmm' absently, nothing more. And although he coaxed, all his patience yielded nothing but the conviction that the Skinners traded on their connection with Floy for whatever reason made sense to them. But Floy was frail and sensitive, and Daisy had a sense of duty because all her life she – and her mother – owed so much to Floy. Everything, she assured him, was now all right, she was sure there would be no repercussions from the regrettable incident of Mr Hutton's accusation that she had endangered his children. What? Because she had climbed the sycamore tree with them. Leaving him to murmur, 'As one does.'

When he put these allusions and evasions together he wasn't satisfied, but whatever was unsaid was family business, and what right had he to trespass there? Besides, there was no hurry; if there was anything he needed to know, all he needed was time.

When Daisy told him about her arrangement with her friend Ellie to open a dancing school, he was so overwhelmed by the thought of her permanence in his life he had no thought of anything else. He said, wholeheartedly, how delighted he was. Of course. She was staying in Chatfield. He could hold onto her, and just for the time being, delight in, endure their charged and unconsummated sexuality.

Travelling in the car with Collier, thinking how he could describe Daisy. He couldn't. She made him think of impossible things: mermaids, Celtic queens, guardian spirits of wells and rivers. Casting no shadow, leaving no footprint. A chimera. 'It should be pronounced shimmera, because that's what it is, does. Onomatopoeia,' he said aloud.

Collier had – at certain moments – given up. His boss, reliably in control, nevertheless had momentary aberrations that were more than his alarming non sequiturs. They didn't affect his work, they were more the faintest vibrations from his private web and, Collier and Annette agreed, only the troops who knew him best sensed them.

Annette said, 'He's bewitched. I'm happy for him.'

'You're jealous.'

'So are you.'

'Right. Live with it.'

'Do we have a choice?'

His occupied life entwined with her lingering time at Fairmead; the future he was beginning to hoard to himself. One morning he telephoned and asked her out to dinner. She said she would look in the engagement book. He smiled, he was never sure when she was playing games; she was just as likely to say, 'I'm judging a bums competition.' But no. 'That'll be fine, I've nothing on.'

They arranged the time, the place, he booked the most superbly expensive restaurant and hotel within reach. When he was ready to leave his flat the doorbell rang. It was Daisy. A leap of dismay – she had come to tell him she was not able to go out with him.

But she was certainly going somewhere: poised in the evening light, in a caressing silk evening coat the colour of topaz, high-heeled strap sandals on sun-tanned feet, coral varnished toenails. He had a breathless comprehension of the exquisite Fairmead dressing-up box, a limitless acceptance of his love for her. He had no words. She stepped in. 'Well, I said I'd nothing on.' Her hands moved with perfect grace, the silk cascaded down her nakedness.

Floy could not have been more delighted about Hunter. 'Such an attractive man and – he looks extremely capable.' Daisy suppressed a screech. Capable, yes, but what did Floy know about *that*? Or was it a guarded reference to Daisy's general absence of efficiency? 'But a policeman's time is very much taken up, just when you've made arrangements for something, he can be called away on duty. Will you mind very much, darling?'

Daisy said gravely that she'd try not to, suspecting that in her head Floy had got her married off already. As for various advantages – one thing was definite, there was nothing like a relationship with a police officer to keep the Skinners away.

Floy entertained Hunter at dinner with sweet ceremony. Clive had brought his friend from the tennis club, Andrew, a young man who knew so many abstruse things about computers he alarmed Floy. Andrew had a charm touched by solemnity and the slightest, beguiling lisp. Clive told Daisy he cultivated the first in order to counterbalance the second, in case people didn't take him seriously; Clive hadn't told him he was wasting his time, because he found the contrast wildly sexy. Andrew was certainly attractive, but next to Hunter became one-dimensional, lisp and all. That he had overlooked Daisy in favour of Clive was something she couldn't imagine should ever have bothered her.

In consultation with Floy, Daisy had organised and cooked, Mrs Lowe officiated, as she often did on social occasions, in black dress and white apron. 'Daisy,' Hunter whispered, 'is this real?'

'Um – yes. No. Does it matter?' which just about summed up everything.

The next day Floy told Daisy with fluttering pleasure that the following week Quill would be coming to spend a few days with them. 'Oh, wouldn't it have been lovely if he'd been here yesterday evening,' Daisy said.

'Absolutely,' Floy agreed with distraction. 'Er, darling, would you mind not mentioning this to anyone, it is just private family business.'

Anyone. The Skinners. 'I can tell Sheldon?'

'Of course,' Floy said in some surprise. Daisy accepted with resignation that her friends were not anyone in the sense that they were not Skinners.

Daisy took him on a circular walk from Fairmead to Bankhill station.

If he had ever had occasion to go there, he'd forgotten; the point was that the original refreshment room ('Oh, shades of *Brief Encounter*,' Daisy breathed) was now a superbly stocked bookshop of railway literature: engineering, social history, industry, politics. Hunter bought an armful of books, Daisy, amazed by his fevered enthusiasm, said, 'I think you ought to know, your eyes have gone as mad as Wile E Coyote's.'

He was unoffended. 'He's always been one of my heroes. He gets blown up, dropped down canyons, run over – but he never gives in. Tell you what, though, one of his wobbly bridges could feel a bloody sight safer than this.' 'This' was the temporary bridge which served while the original was being reconstructed. They stood hugged together; on the embankment below white moon daisies tangled with high purple foxgloves, from somewhere the scent of orange blossom drifted, a solitary thrush poured out its liquid song while the evening turned to apricot and azure around them. She was apologetic about her claim that this was the Festival of Britain Emett Railway because she'd never seen it and that happened before she was born; Hunter said he could remember it, just, and she was probably right.

She was serious about the moment when the material and metaphysical connection to Bankhill found expression: the railway lines travelling, disappearing from past to present to future, as if she was in this place for no more than an intake of breath, a glance, a sigh. He said, 'Oh, no, I'm not letting go,' and holding her slender body, encompassing her with his strength, his protection, he told her about the first time he saw her, and thought she was a ghost.

'What?' She looked amused, disbelieving.

'It was evening, I was driving down Palmerston...' He tried to describe the effect she had on him, how she had vanished.

She said, 'Well of course, that's what ghosts do. I never imagined I'd be mistaken for a revenant. Horrid word.'

Yes, but to make her feel better, 'It doesn't necessarily mean a ghost. It's also someone returned from exile.'

'Ah, that's what I feel when I'm away from Bankhill. Exiled. I never ever want to leave it.'

He intended she never would.

They were curled up on the sofa in his flat. His 'luxury apartment' as the estate agents would have it, was a Sixties built block, an impressive façade, an interior of the most unwelcoming minimalism. When he said something about this, she politely answered that, well, it was a bit... 'Darling, we can buy —' but she wasn't listening. In the enchantment of her presence he had only just realised how she had been subdued. 'What is it?'

After a while she told him. She had telephoned her mother (finding a reason, not saying she wanted to tell her about this marvellous man in her life).

'I just wanted to say hallo, see how she was getting on, but... This guy she's been living with for five years, he's quite sweet...'

'Yes?'

'She's done a bunk. She won't have gone off on her own, there'll be another man. Manuel's awfully fed up, called her all sorts of names. Who can blame him?'

'You mean, you don't know where she is?'

'There's nothing new about that. Give her her due, she always knew I was safe with Floy or Quill or Clive's family. She's been doing this all my life. I've lost track of her for months on end. Once it was two years —'

His amazed realisation of the difference between his background and hers.

* * *

He called to take her to Merlin Edge for a morning's walk, then to Knutsford for lunch at the Belle Époque. Floy opened the door to him, poised always between charm and confusion: the confusion on this occasion because Daisy was next door watering Grace's pot plants. She looked uncertainly towards the telephone alcove, murmured she could, er… Hunter said certainly not, let the poor things get the required dousing; so they sat in the garden room together. He said, 'I thought Daisy said Grace had come home.'

'Yes, and it's delightful to have her back, but she's just – what do you say? Touched base? Now she's in Edinburgh, grandchild's christening, unmissable. She'll certainly be back in time to see Quill. Are you sure you don't want me to let Daisy know you're here? She never keeps people waiting, she's quite ready —'

He said no, he was early, he didn't need small talk, he'd make use of this time, sure Floy would overlook his directness, she no doubt regarded it as the province of chaps. 'She was rather upset about her mother going off with another man. Did she tell you?'

'Oh yes, but that's the pattern of her life, I'm afraid. Madelaine – her mother – is delightful but so mercurial. Daisy accepts it quite philosophically. As a child, such a thin, sweet little scrap of a girl; when Madelaine left her here it used to break her heart – although she pretended everything was all right. She was always making the best of things, eager to help…' She talked on, unwittingly building a picture of Daisy trailed here and there, discarded, gathered up again, passed around. It occurred to him that Daisy had endured neglect amounting to abuse. But there was always the saving grace, the welcome here, the protectiveness, the unstinting giving: Daisy must have what all the other girls had, what Clive had. Good clothes, dancing classes, a bicycle, riding lessons.

There was something in all this on the edge of his attention, he didn't identify it until later. When Daisy had talked, reluctantly, of Edward being farmed out till he was old enough to take off on his own – her life, give or take details, was a mirror image of his.

* * *

Clive phoned Daisy, said if she was not too distracted by the madness of a love affair with a great big rough policeman – 'Oh, jealous, jealous,' she cooed – could she collect Mrs Twemlowe's bits and pieces. She had to think for a moment – concede she was distracted, she had completely forgotten. She walked around to the Quadrant, had a friendly chat with Josie, whom she hadn't encountered for years but who knew all sorts of things about her. From Big John? 'Of course,' Josie said, 'you don't know what a ferment of gossip those bloody Skinners are.'

'I do, and most of it's inaccurate.'

'Oh, they just make things up. Except about you and that lovely copper.'

'All right, but you've got your own lovely man. Hand over the goods and quit stalling.'

Josie had them at the house on Balmoral, which she was keeping an eye on prior to putting it up for sale.

'Would you like to bring them round to Fairmead and have a drink with us? Floy would love to see you, you can tell her about your mum.'

Josie called round the next evening, bringing with her a daunting range of boxes, envelopes, scrap books, journals. After she had gone, Daisy groaned, 'Why did I start all this?' and lugged everything up to the games room. Afterwards, driven by conscience, and when she had nothing pressing to do, she sorted through them.

Chapter Twenty-One

When Daisy had – minimal – attention to spare from Hunter over the next few days, she registered the ambivalence of Floy's attitude towards Quill's visit: the bewildering alternation of anxiety and relief. She was hiding something, Daisy was sure... Then she thought what she had hidden from Floy – a positive mountain of deceit. Quill would bring his own reassurance, perhaps she would find the opportunity to have a discreet talk with him.

When the day arrived everything was swept aside in the happiness of anticipation. The guest room gleamed, welcoming; a simple but delicious supper was prepared, Veuve Clicquot (Quill's favourite) in the fridge, Floy and Daisy, at six thirty, relaxed and ready for the evening.

At seven thirty they told each other that anything could have delayed him; perhaps the ferry had been late, perhaps he'd had a puncture and found it difficult to get to a phone, or...

By eight thirty Floy was strung out with tension. Daisy had to do something. She telephoned Mrs Caffrey, Quill's housekeeper, to be told with strenuous cheerfulness that himself had left for the ferry in plenty of time, plenty of time, there'd be nothing more than a little hold-up somewhere...

Then something was awry, a trembling note, 'But – Mr Edward rang earlier on, only I had... I was...'

An inward groan, oh, God, he's back is he?

Mrs Caffrey was Quill's treasure, he would not allow her to be upset or inconvenienced. Daisy had seen at first hand the patience he exercised, making Edward behave decently, and for one so mild, the firmness – it seemed he could protect others, but not himself, from Edward's moods.

'It's all right, Mrs Caffrey,' she said gently. 'Just tell me.'

'He was wanting to speak to himself and himself had instructed me to say he'd not be in but back later.'

'Of course,' Daisy said, bracingly sensible although she could make no sense of it at all, but needed to keep Mrs Caffrey on a straight course.

'And Mr Edward was not – he shouted, Miss Donovan, he shouted – he's not there is he? He – he called me a lying bitch.'

'Oh, I'm so sorry, just try not to be upset.'

'No, that's what himself always says.'

'Quite right.' Daisy spent some time soothing, reassuring, trying to sound confident. Afterwards, the same dissembling, reported to Floy that Mrs Caffrey had no news, 'there's been some drama with Quill and Edward.'

Floy said, puzzled, 'I understood they were no longer…it was not any more a relationship —' turned away, delicately unengaged…

For the next hour they discussed every possibility: he had changed his mind; called somewhere else on the way and been delayed… The word accident was not spoken. Daisy rang Clive, but got only his answerphone. She rang Andrew, with the same result.

She was in charge of dinner, when any guest was travelling a distance she always gave a leeway of an hour either side, even so, standing in the kitchen, amongst the forlorn preparations, she had a sick feeling: it was so unlike Quill not to find some way of letting them know where he was, if he'd had some reason for altering his plans. She longed for Hunter, but he was spending the evening with friends, tactfully saying that he looked forward to meeting Quill but their reunion was something to keep to themselves.

She phoned Mrs Caffrey again, garnered information Mrs Caffrey had overlooked in her upset about Edward. 'Miss Daisy, I'm sorry, I'd not be being such a fool. I should have said, I couldn't but pull meself togither.'

'Not at all, I understand.' Casually, 'We haven't heard from Quill yet and I forgot to ask before, what ferry did he take?'

'Twas the eleven ten.'

'Oh – er – so early.'

'Why yes, Miss, I should have been telling you, only I was upset about —'

Daisy made soothing and encouraging sounds, heart lightening, here was a long awaited explanation.

'You know how when he's passing through Conway he takes the chance to lunch with Colonel Denwright if he can. Did he not tell Miss Floy?'

'Possibly, she might have, um, misunderstood.'

So that would be the reason for the earlier ferry. It didn't answer the big question, though. She got the Colonel's number, phoned. After a barked, 'What? What?' he identified her, fell into the gossipy delight of an old man no one listens to very much. 'Little Daisy, little Daisy. Of course, Quill was speaking of you.' She had to hold her patience through preambles and digressions, through old hunting episodes when she was no more than a slip of a girl. 'We were only saying at luncheon, you were so often thrown straight into ditches, do you know what Quill said?'

Yes, wearily, she could recite it silently him:

'Help on the seat of your jodhpurs.'

She allowed him his reedy tee-hee, and a fit of coughing for good measure, then, persevering, found out when Quill arrived, when he left, that he was on his way straight to Chatfield. She worked out that if the Colonel's timing was right, and she had no doubt it was (*meticulous old buffer* – Quill had once described him), then Quill should have arrived at Fairmead around about four o'clock.

'Quill wanted to stay longer, but he had things to do. Don't see old friends often enough. And how is Floy? Had that op, dodgy things those.'

'She's awfully well thank you —' insane with worry. It seemed so crass, trampling on reminiscences and courtesies, but she had to ring off, and think.

Quill had left because he had things to do. What things? Where did he go?

Daisy grazed, with small, desperate appetite, an idea of keeping up her strength – for what? Floy would eat nothing. Relentlessly, the situation moved beyond anxiety towards unspoken embarrassment.

How many times Quill had visited when she was not there she had no way of knowing, but over so many years – just beyond memory, finding and losing her place in the Mannering existence – there had to be an occasion when Floy referred to Edward 'going elsewhere'. Perhaps the naïve euphemism was employed at a time when Daisy was too young to know Quill and Edward shared a bedroom, or understood what that meant. Later, when she did, she suffered – not from her own crassness – but from Floy's embarrassment. And was it then, or some other occasion, when Floy said, with strained determination and obviously in response to some imbecilic question, 'I prefer Edward not to spend any time here at all. It's a personal feeling.' The 'personal feeling' was that, nothing more – no explanation. Daisy then obliquely received the understanding that had there been any way to avoid it, Floy would have said nothing at all. Perhaps, to her, Edward was still an insolent boy, perhaps she had managed to expunge from her mind his long association with Quill; certainly there was no need for either of them to voice their assumption that Quill would have been accompanied by Edward, that on arrival at Bankhill he would go – somewhere, stay somewhere, possibly with his own family.

Floy was so close to hysteria she dare not mention the name of Skinner, the thought of doing something herself, underhandedly, made her cringe. She could imagine the crude glee that would meet even the most tentative query – Quillie you don't know where he is – well why you bloody telling me? Likewise – or worse – asking for Edward; whoever she spoke to would be obstructive through either stupidity or malice.

She delayed too long, until midnight, then it was too late to phone anyone; she insisted they went to bed.

Early next morning she phoned Hunter at Talbot Way. He was unavailable. Of course, that was his job, his duty, to be unavailable in trivial disasters in order to deal with larger law-threatening ones.

The day was dislocated. It was hours before she contacted Clive, he was out of his office, she left urgent messages with his secretary to telephone Fairmead. At last, he phoned, sounding harassed. He listened to her news, expressed surprise – he had heard nothing from Quill – said, 'Daisy, are you sure Floy's got the right date, she's a bit, nowadays, you know…'

It was a thought. Daisy had not been home when Quill phoned to make the arrangement. Surreptitiously she consulted the desk diary, questioned Floy in a conversational way, was more or less convinced that Floy had put down the right time on the right date.

Floy, up much earlier than usual, claimed to have slept but her face told another story. She was perfectly dressed, carefully made up, and calm; this was a crisis and in a crisis one behaved well. She made a dignified little speech. 'Daisy, I'm afraid I was no help last night, you're just as worried as I am. I'm quite sure there's some rational explanation for all this. Perhaps, heaven knows how, there was something misunderstood in our arrangements.'

It was one of Mrs Lowe's days in. Daisy explained as much as she thought made sense, but it was beginning to recede from her.

Mrs Lowe said, 'Someone called, asking for Sir Quill, I said we didn't expect him till the evening. He asked what time, I said six thirty to seven.'

'Do you know who he was, did he give his name?'

'No, he just rang off. I couldn't place his voice.'

Leaving Floy in the company of Mrs Lowe, Daisy took herself to Talbot Way. Hunter was not there; she folded in on herself, defeated. Annette came out to Reception to see her. 'Hey, Daisy, you look all in.'

'I just wanted to speak to Sheldon, but he's not available.'

'He's at Headquarters today. What's up?'

'Oh, no, it's nothing.'

'Nothing. You've got trouble written all over you. Come on, you can trust me.'

'Annette, how do you go about finding someone missing?'

'Who?'

She had only begun to tell her about Quill when the desk sergeant leaned across the counter, called, 'Annette, DS Crabbe's looking for you.'

'How looking?'

'Fire coming out of his nostrils.'

'Oh, hell. Daisy, I'll have to go —'

'Of course —'

'But you could do this without me, you know, you could make it official, fill out a Missing Persons Report.'

'Annette, I couldn't. Floy —'

'Talk to her about it. OK?'

A message scribbled by Annette to Hunter read, 'Daisy. Crisis? Phone.' – brevity and question mark so perfectly conveying that any crisis to do with Daisy was problematical but if it wasn't he'd give her hell for not letting him know.

He phoned Daisy at lunchtime, heard her deliberately keeping her voice steady, 'Sheldon, we're rather worried. Quill didn't turn up yesterday and we can't find anyone who knows where he is.'

'No one at all?' He went through all contacts and probabilities, she told him about Quill breaking his journey at Conway to lunch with the Colonel. 'After that, I can't find anyone who's heard from him. Annette told me about a missing persons report, but I wouldn't dare to, not without asking Floy and I haven't had time to speak to her —' for which she was cowardly thankful. Grace, forewarned by Daisy of the bewildering situation, had called in during the morning and, to distract Floy, carried her off to lunch with friends. Daisy knew where to contact her, stayed at Fairmead, waiting for the phone to ring.

Hunter had said often enough to Daisy that he cherished the Mannerings' dottiness, he could hardly be expected to take seriously the non-appearance of a near mythical being. She had done her best to explain to him Quill's ivory tower existence; Hunter could not help but see him lodged in the interstice of a long discarded society. But, Daisy insisted, he observed the most minute everyday courtesies, he would never have put them both to so much worry if he could have prevented it. Floy was his closest, cherished relative.

That woman made of silver filigree, or cut glass or something equally brittle – how had she survived so long? She seemed not so much incapable of making any decision apart from what to wear or plant, but to have jettisoned even the necessity; concealed within her genuine sweetness and charm, the tenacity of the self-deluded enabled her to keep herself cocooned in the only place she could function – the eternally innocent world of Just William.

Daisy said that Floy and Quill between them had made the arrangements; that being the case – including as it did a previously overlooked Colonel Blimp – it seemed to Hunter the possibilities of disarray were limitless.

He said reassuring and encouraging things in the short amount of time he had, told her that if anything further occurred to go to Talbot Way and speak to Annette or James. Wasn't James away on holiday, she reminded him in a small voice.

'He'll be back tomorrow. I'm sorry, darling, I'll be tied up till late tonight. Could you come round to me then? Get a taxi.'

'I wish I could, but I really shouldn't leave Floy.'

'No, of course not. I'll speak to you tomorrow.'

His view was that Quill was a rational adult, wealthy, free to go wherever he wished, and some nudge of intuition had always insinuated that Quill led a life too separate for Floy – and sometimes Daisy – to grasp. What they saw as romantic distance, to Quill could very well be necessary defence.

Not that he could say anything of the sort to Daisy.

Chapter Twenty-Two

The body was found in north Chatfield by an all-night garage attendant on his way home, in a curiously sinister area called Cut End. A truncated portion of the elaborate and once thriving canal commerce, this had collapsed to its ultimate degradation: a slimy basin, its centre a mass of stagnant water and deposit, its periphery here and there treadable. The stink was stomach-turning, guaranteed to keep anyone away; the ownership of the area had been in dispute for years, it was no one's responsibility. The entrance, which was little more than a crevice linked by a passage to a frantic street of clubs, pubs, and sex shops, was narrow enough to discourage anyone from using it as a parking space or dumping ground for stolen vehicles.

The garage attendant, passing the opening to the passageway, had been knocked down by two youths running for their lives; as he fell, he saw them throw something away. He got to his feet and picked it up; it was a wallet they had obviously just rifled. With their flight the place grew quiet, there was no one else about, he ventured down towards the wharf, saw the body and called the police.

When Hunter arrived, a Scene of Crime Officer was at work and Sergeant Bale was waiting for him.

The victim, an elderly man, had been bludgeoned about the head. One look told Hunter there was no life left in that fine old silver-haired skull.

'Do we know who he is?'

'Sir Aquilla Mannering, resident in Eire.'

He couldn't speak. So many forces drew together.

Sir Aquilla. Daisy's uncle Quill.

'Know him, sir?'

'No, no, not personally, but I know of him. Sorry, what were you saying?'

Bale explained about the youths and the wallet. 'They didn't have time to empty it of everything before they legged it, went for the obvious, cash and credit cards. There's a well, I'd have said business card but according to,' Sergeant Bale lowered his voice, nodding towards the approaching Detective Sergeant James Collier, 'according to him, it's a visiting card. The victim was his uncle.'

'What?' Hunter stared. 'James, good God. Your uncle?'

There was the distant hum of the city around them, its jarring music, the detritus in the gutters, the pell-mell of heedless, cheap, striving existence, and the over-riding smell of Cut End, a corpse of enterprise, bearing a corpse. The thought came to Hunter that if his valued sergeant had suffered a bereavement this was just about the worst place it could happen.

'No, no,' James looked away, an almost irritable movement concealing inner distress. 'No, I called him that.' He turned back, collected, but in the harsh lights his young face was momentarily bleak. 'Uncle – it was a courtesy title, I knew him when I was little. I'd lost touch, but years ago my parents were friends with the Mannerings. In Bankhill.'

'James, if you're going to find this hard to cope with —'

'No, guv. I haven't seen him for years, I was fond of him and I respected him. I want to find out who did this.'

'I had no idea you had some connection, perhaps if I'd asked you — But, you've been on leave…'

'Ask me what?' Collier gave him a puzzled look. 'What are you talking about, guv?'

'About Quill – did you know he was Floy Mannering's cousin?'

'Well – now you mention it, I suppose I did. I haven't seen him since I was a boy. God, how awful for her, for Daisy —'

'It's not just that, James. He was coming to stay with Floy and Daisy, Wednesday evening. But he went missing. Daisy spent all yesterday trying to trace him.'

Collier looked baffled. 'Didn't she report it?'

'No – thing is, she wouldn't do it without asking Floy, and she was getting round to that. I thought, I just didn't give it any weight, you know how…' Hunter gave up, swore comprehensively, with invention.

When all the necessary jobs were apportioned and under way, Hunter spoke to Collier again. 'I'll have to go to Fairmead and tell Daisy – she'll have to break the news to Floy, I don't want this getting to them before I do.'

Collier said, 'Would you like me – or Annette —'

'No, James, you'll be more use here, but I'll take Annette with me.'

As they drove to Fairmead, Annette asked, 'Did he have a special reason for coming here? James says these last few years he's seldom left Ireland.'

Two of his best troops, they worked intuitively together, in this instance they'd got there before him, and not just by swapping notes; this was specific, their shared links to Bankhill. James had known Quill, he might know of possible contacts who could provide useful information.

When he told Annette Quill had intended to visit Hugh Stephenson at the Manor, she said at once, 'Oh, yes, Stephenson's Studio. Before my time, but, you know my parents, grandmother —'

'Ah, the Madam shop,' Hunter breathed.

'Yes, well, when we visited Grandmother, went with her to her friends, their homes were sort of – embalmed in the Thirties – and Stephenson's had been there since then. Hugh was the second generation photographer, he started the local photography club. Go in any house in Bankhill, there wasn't one that didn't have its portrait of cherished tots, they were as much of the time as Clarice Cliff and bevelled mirrors on chains hanging from picture rails.'

'Were you one – a cherished tot?'

'Well, yes, but as a *mere babe*. So he's in the Manor now? They can be a pretty spry lot there, you know, ancient ladies playing bridge like fiends and drinking gin.'

'Daisy said he's had a stroke, he won't be so spry. I want you to go and see him, you and James. Find out if Quill went there instead of straight to Fairmead, if he did, did they talk and what about?'

At Fairmead, Annette tactfully lingered, while Hunter held Daisy, her fierce helplessness, a sorrow as much on Floy's behalf as her own.

In the beautiful lounge hall Floy sat in the contained posture of grief: straight back, hands clasped, eyes far away on the unknowable past. She accepted Hunter's condolences but he could see she was shut in, not functioning. Annette supplied grace notes; she was so good at it he frequently referred to her as Ms Grace Notes.

There were questions, essential procedures. Time was consumed by mundane matters. Floy, held together by a lifetime's good behaviour, had been overcome by a state approaching catatonia; occasionally she murmured, 'I'm sorry, I can't seem to...' Then Daisy would take her hand, say something sensible and gentle, reinstate her place in the conversation.

Hunter put aside his personal judgement of himself as a trampling hippopotamus, segued into his professional persona, 'You expected Quill here at six thirty, Floy?'

She gave him a bewildered look. Daisy answered, 'Yes,' for her.

'How did you make the arrangement? By telephone?' Another silent look, then a nod.

Annette turned to Daisy. 'You told Mr Hunter that he stopped off at Conway to have lunch with an old friend.'

'Yes, Colonel Denwright.'

When Hunter asked for the Colonel's address she looked rather wild for an instant. 'What? Why?' Annette who knew the supreme Hunterism was in operation – *assume nothing, verify everything* – reassured her. 'We'll want to send someone to see the old boy, check on what time Quill left, have a chat with him, there might be something that could jog his memory about where Quill would go.'

Daisy said yes, she could see that, but he still had plenty of time, and could easily have made it for six thirty. Floy spoke suddenly, 'He'd be tired, the journey, driving to Dun Laoghaire then from Holyhead, and he's not awfully strong.'

'Might he have gone straight to the nursing home?' Hunter asked.

Floy frowned. Daisy looked suddenly helpless, 'Oh, Floy, I never thought – I should have phoned – I could now —'

Hunter said, 'No, leave it, Daisy, we're going to do that.'

Annette, gently persistent with Floy, 'He had friends, long

standing contacts in Bankhill. Might he have stayed with one of them last night?'

When she shook her head, Daisy said, 'One or two, not many really. And he just wouldn't do that, he'd wait till another day to visit and take Floy – that's what he always did.'

Floy said, 'We share old friends...'

'Anyway,' Daisy added, 'I've asked everyone I can think of.'

'Did he say anything to Clive?' Hunter asked her.

'No. I left a message on his answerphone yesterday, but he didn't pick it up till this morning. He's as much in the dark as we are.'

Hunter said, 'Floy, who do we have to notify? Who is Sir Aquilla's next of kin?'

She thought, momentarily reclaimed from her emotional wasteland. 'I suppose, consanguinity, it must be me.' She gave Daisy a perplexed look.

Daisy said, 'It must, you're first cousins. And he never married, or had any children that we know of.' She explained to Hunter, 'Quill was the youngest of six brothers, they're all dead now.'

There would be time enough to discover who inherited from Quill, Daisy would not know, possibly Floy didn't either.

When they left, he looked back to where Daisy stood at the white gates, in the morning sunlight, raising her hand in a delicate farewell as eloquent as an entreaty across the distance that separated them.

Their helplessness came to him. How could they make sense of what had overtaken them? His instinct told him that they unknowingly had, if not the answer, then the means of leading him towards it through the private motivations, the web of circumstances that had brought about this tragedy.

Annette said, 'Why have I got an awful feeling the Skinners are in this somewhere?'

'Don't let your imagination run away with you.' Hunter reached for his car phone. 'I'm going to tell James to meet us halfway at the Dragon car park, then you can both get round to the Manor Nursing Home. If there's anything significant, report to me directly.'

As they pulled into the car park, James was following. Hunter said, 'He's upset about Quill. Look out for him, Annette.'

'Please, please, please, don't take him off the investigation.'

So James had told her that. Of course. 'No, no, you know I value his professionalism. But I haven't time to spend hand holding. Not that I could very well, anyway.'

Getting out of the car, she gave him her wordless, sideways look.

'Don't you dare say it, girl.'

As he drove away, the accusation in her head. *All right, so we're both in love with you.*

How could a man so clever just not know it?

Chapter Twenty-Three

At the evening briefing, the first information established that Sir Aquilla had not met his death where his body was found. In Brute Force's crude summary, *he'd not been topped where he'd been dumped.* Nevertheless, enquiries and an area search were on-going.

Hunter said, 'We know he disembarked at Holyhead at twelve forty-nine. An hour later lunched with a friend at Conway, turned up at Manor Nursing Home shortly before five – it's at Gortway Park, just off the Wrexham road. James and Annette will have something to say about that in a moment. He stayed there in the company of an old friend, Hugh Stephenson, and left at six thirty approx.'

Sergeant Bale asked, 'Do we have any eye-witnesses to him leaving the Manor car park?'

'No. One of your men out on patrol found his car early this morning.'

'That's right, Hasley Green industrial estate.' Everyone knew it, industry long fled, it stood in its own desolation, scarred and dilapidated, so easy of access its only purpose now was for disposal, the first place anyone looked for a missing vehicle – even a missing person, there were enough of those around, making use of the wreckage that had once been buildings. 'It appeared overnight, must have been late on because the vandals had only just got to it. We asked around but nobody saw anything, nobody ever does round there. It's being tested by SOCO. I think we'll find the victim's body was in it from the time he left the Manor on Wednesday evening until some time early this morning when he was taken to Cut End, then the car driven to Hasley Green and left for us to find.'

Someone asked, 'Why two locations? Car in one place, body in another.'

'The car because at Hasley it'd be found as soon as it's left. Cut End's so seldom used the body could have been there for days if those lads hadn't been fooling about, even then they'd not have been likely to tell anyone if the garage attendant hadn't seen them. But a car, left there, everyone'd take a look at that. Which suggests the murderer knew what he was doing.'

Sergeant Bale said, 'That doesn't necessarily mean he'd be local, but he'd definitely had to have knowledge of the area. Nobody'd just chance on that passageway, you'd have to know you could reverse a car up it, just enough room to squeeze round to the boot, lift the body out and dump it, then – away.'

Mary Clegg said, 'The two locations not only confused us but gave him time to cover his tracks, get away.'

The literally minded DC Paul Evans asked, 'Sir, does it have to be a him?' Evans' thought processes were ponderous, articulated with deliberation, it was claimed people had actually fallen asleep during one of his sentences.

A momentary pause. 'Your point?' Hunter asked.

'The victim was a frail man, small bones. A woman could have not only murdered him but lifted his body onto the dump, an athletic, strong woman.' In the silence of a thought provoked, Hunter considered hefty Skinner women, cleaning, working in the bottle factory, heaving cartons about in storerooms – he doubted if put together they had the necessary intelligence to plan, organise and carry out such a crime.

'Just well, it's a possibility to consider.'

Hunter agreed it was, and he'd consider it.

Another question, 'What about this friend he visited at the Manor, could he tell us anything?'

Hunter glanced at Annette and Collier, who had raced each other to bring the news to him.

'We spoke to him, for all the good it did. It wasn't possible to make any meaningful connection,' Annette said. He had talked at length about matters so long ago they might, or might not be verifiable, and even so, appeared to have no bearing on the present enquiry. He frequently mentioned Quill, but this was in terms of a lost history, and whatever had been said between them was now undiscoverable. 'We told him Quill had had an accident, he started to get upset, insisting it wasn't Quill, and it wasn't Clive. By then he was pretty well exhausted. The doctor asked us to leave it until tomorrow and if the situation hadn't changed to, maybe, try to speak to him again. We asked, but he's not well enough to be questioned.'

Hunter said, 'But, somebody else called at the Manor while Sir Aquilla was visiting his friend.'

James said, 'Clive Mannering. He's Sir Aquilla's nephew, has a publishing firm in the old Courier building on Manchester Square. Lives in Chatfield, at Chambers.'

An appreciative murmur, 'Lucky for some.' Everyone knew Chambers, the sublimely Gothic Victorian hotel, its tiled corridors, tiers of floors of opulently plastered rooms, basements, attics, balconies; all so long neglected, even its courtyard and stables dilapidated, rented out to struggling ventures. Then came the surge of inner city regeneration; restored, redeveloped, Chambers was the last word in elegance and expense.

'He told the receptionist that it was important Sir Aquilla got in touch with him. He then made a phone call on the Manor's phone, and left. We checked. The number he called was his own.'

Someone murmured, 'Why would he do that?'

James shrugged, 'The phone's in its own alcove across the hall. The receptionist couldn't hear what he said, just that he didn't speak for more than a couple of minutes.'

Mr Clive Mannering had some explaining to do.

Hunter gave thought who to send to interview Clive Mannering, Annette and James were tied up. He decided on DC Martin Barlow, a recent transferee from North Yorkshire and so keen to prove he was up to it you could cut yourself on his shadow. New to the territory, he would have a fresh eye on everything going on and so young he functioned like a sponge, soaking up, retaining impressions. He teamed Mary Clegg with him, not only because of her copper-bottomed common sense, but because she had the advantage of already meeting Clive Mannering. Briefly enough, and in spite of her dazzled reaction at the time, she was more than equipped to gauge any changes in his manner.

Chambers. Behind curlicued iron railings and gently spreading foliage, they confronted Clive's gleamingly brass accoutred front door.

PC Barlow glanced round, murmured, 'Wow.'

'Isn't it just?' Mary whispered.

She had seen Clive just the once – an elegant, sweetly teasing man, now, his grief contained, he politely invited them in to sit down. Was it a sitting room – or area? Space gave way to space that dictated its own function: dining, drinking, studying, relaxing. He gave her an abstracted but genuine smile of recognition, 'Hallo, I met you at Fairmead, didn't I?'

'Oh, yes?' Mary said, as if the encounter had slipped her memory.

DC Barlow said, 'Mr Mannering, you understand this is necessary procedure. We'd like you to tell us what you were doing yesterday from six thirty p.m. This is purely for purposes of elimination.'

Clive answered that he was here, had brought work home, devoted the evening to it.

They took the questioning in turns, subtly altering the tempo.

'Did you have any phone calls?'

'There might have been – I had a shower, couldn't hear from there.'

'Did you check for messages?'

'Not till the next day. There was one from Miss Donovan, she's staying with —'

'Yes, we know about Miss Donovan's call. Any others?'

'No.'

'So, you were here, alone. Did you go out at any time?'

He thought. Barlow asked sharply could he not remember. Sir.

Yes, he was trying to think what time. Later on, he went out for a walk, he'd been working all evening, needed some fresh air to clear his head.

'A walk? And this was?'

'I can't be exact. Ten thirty, eleven.'

'Did you meet anyone, speak to anyone?'

'No, if there was anyone I'd be too pre-occupied to notice them.'

Beneath his control he was showing and mastering some strain, striving to cope with the changing directions of the questioning.

'And the next day, when you checked your messages, there was just the one from Miss Donovan, no one else?'

'No.'

DC Barlow repeated, No, and let the negative linger. Said briskly, 'I think that's all for the moment. Thank you, Mr Mannering.'

With the air of everything satisfactorily settled, they left.

Clive's residence – how could it be called anything else? – stood on a corner. They had not parked before the frontage, but on the road that gave access to his garage and courtyard. Wherever you were around here, the surroundings were impressive.

They compared notes. Barlow said, 'He's not telling the truth.'

'He's telling some of it.'

'What bits? Come on, Hunter —'

'Mr Hunter to you. You're new here, yes, pushy – aren't we all.'

'Right, sorry.' New, yes, but he'd picked up vibrations of devotion. 'Just, Mr Hunter said you'd met him before.'

'OK, hardly counts as *meeting*.' Those shining moments at Fairmead... She had to tell it as she knew. 'Obviously his manner's different, what else d'you expect? A close relative's met a violent death. But, as well, he's – ill at ease. There's something not right there, but I don't... Was it when you asked him if he went out?'

'Yeah. He deliberately hesitated – breathing space.'

'So. Only one thing to do. Check did he go out – between ten and eleven, he said. Ask around.'

They agreed on their line of questioning, unspecific, flexible. Had anyone been out between ten and eleven the previous night and seen anyone, known or unknown, walking about?

They quartered the area, the hushed, handsome dwellings, the courtyards and designer plots. The end result, no one had seen him but a neighbour offered the information that he'd been going indoors much earlier, round about seven and heard a car revving noisily outside Clive's house. After that, they spoke to another neighbour who had gone out but much earlier, taking his dog for a walk. How much earlier? Sevenish. Yes, he'd heard revving, there had been a car at the corner, making a terrible racket, and driving off in a screeching hurry. He was too far away to see who was driving it, if it was a man or a woman. It was a BMW. Did it belong to the people at the corner house? 'No. Publisher chappy. He's got a Jaguar.'

There was a faint dismay, instantly dismissed, on Clive's face as he opened the door to find them once more on the step.

Mr Mannering, if we can impose on you again…thank you, that's very good of you…we've been making enquiries locally in case anyone saw anyone or anything out of the usual…and two of your neighbours tell us that there was a car revving very loudly outside your house on Wednesday evening. Some of your near neighbours heard it, one of them saw the car, it was a BMW…

When Clive didn't reply, Barlow said, 'You know, of course, that Sir Aquilla's car is a BMW.'

'Is it? He must have changed it, perhaps he told me, I don't recall. He changes his car once a year, and I haven't seen him for over two years; then it was a Rover.'

Mary's vivid recollection of him at Fairmead, his boyish good humour – this was a restrained man, attentive, his expression deliberately closed.

DC Barlow said, 'A Rover, I see,' glanced at Mary conspicuously making notes. 'Did Sir Aquilla call on you about seven on Wednesday evening?'

Clive sighed, restrained impatience. 'No, I told you, I had no callers all evening.'

'Right, sir. If you wouldn't mind making a statement to that effect. We can do it now, save you coming to the station.'

'Really, do I have to?'

'Helps oil the wheels, sir. Then we can all get on with our jobs,' DC Barlow said, cheerfully philosophical.

Hunter, reading through the report, pondered Clive's claim about not having seen Quill for over two years. What had Daisy said about Quill's last visit? He telephoned, asked. Just before last Christmas. 'I wasn't here, but I know he stayed with Floy. Is it important?'

'We don't know what is important and what isn't, darling. Just have to cover all possibilities.'

'Of course.'

Later, Mary Clegg shared refreshment in the canteen with George Withers, the community policeman. He was Hunter's oldest friend, they had been together from snotty, toddling years through brawling adolescence to their first years as recruits. The time was too long, too established to let anything like difference in rank come between them. George, securely married, with progeny that filled him with pride, dearly wanted Hunter to settle down with a nice girl. So many had come and gone. He had now decided Daisy would more than do. He was astonished when Mary told him about the Mannerings' distant connection with the Skinners. He repeated the name with a world of disbelief.

'Yes, I know. Don't ask me how, someone married someone else – but not the Chatfield Skinners, the ones from the Easton estate.'

George knew them too, small time, nuisance more than criminal. 'Do you think they're implicated in the murder of this Sir whatsit?'

Mary sighed. 'Who can say? It's all up for grabs. The thing is, a car, with a body in it, disappears from the Manor. Then, the body turns up – how many hours later at Cut End. Where was it all that time?'

They talked it over, agreed it had to be in reasonable disposing distance of the city for both car and body to be found on the Friday morning.

Slowly, turning it over in his mind George reminded her of a raid on a lock-up behind Donkey Alley, stolen goods were found. 'He went down, while he's inside he's passed the garage on to a cousin, Nosey Skinner. Really nasty piece of work, that one, GBH and the rest.'

'Well, then. A lock up? Thanks, George.'

He didn't need to say, 'Worth a try.' Mary was a bright girl.

On patrol with Brute Force, she insisted they make for Donkey Alley. His objection was unequivocal, 'Bloody why?'

'Lock-up,' she said.

Lock-ups, he pointed out, were bloody everywhere. It was true, everywhere in the back streets and overlooked reaches of Chatfield. 'What's it to do with?'

'Death of Sir Aquilla.'

'Sodding bloody Sir aristocrat, are we supposed to pull out all the —'

'Just shut it and go there.'

With Brute Force's reluctant assistance, she ranged Donkey Alley, talking to anyone within reach, most of whom wanted nothing to do with her: hardly surprising in 'the landscape of despair' as Hunter had once put it. Through sheer tenacity, she found Annie – or rather, rediscovered her, she'd helped her through a bad time with a violent partner. 'Hey, Annie, you ok?'

'Yeah, on me way to work —' a jerk of the head towards the steamed windows of a caff that sold delicious platefuls of life-threatening food.

They talked for a while, Mary aware of, and ignoring, Brute Force's heaving impatience. 'What you doing round here, then, Mary?'

'Keep it to yourself, but we might be interested in a lock-up round there, at present used by Nosey Skinner.'

'Yeah? Funny thing, the other night when I'd finished and on me way home, this posh car driving in there – honest to God, no one'd believe me if I said owt. Not that I'm going to. It was, I'm telling you, suthink you just don't see round here.'

'Really, Annie?'

'Yeh, God's strewth. "What's this then?" I says to meself. So I hangs about, and then this geezer comes out the garridge – honest to God – you don't get any of them round here. Not as I've ever seen. A real looker, and his clothes, just locks up doors and walks away.'

'It wasn't Nosey's car?'

'What? He should be so lucky. I clocked this feller as he walks past, right past me. Really good looking, really proper feller.'

'Had you ever seen him before?'

'I wish. Nah.' Words died, revived, 'Really proper feller.'

After pressure Mary had a minimal description, six feet, fair-haired. 'Did you ask Nosey who he was?'

'What – and get me face rearranged? No thanks.'

'Would you recognise him again? Would you identify him?

'You've just had your answer to that, love.'

It seemed to Daisy unforgivably callous to telephone Mrs Caffrey with the news that her dear employer was dead – murdered – dumped in a terrible place. She talked to Clive, they agreed Floy needed them both, and they would neither of them be any use in Ireland, and Clive was in touch with Quill's solicitor. There was only one person she could trust to speak to Mrs Caffrey, Quill's strong and long loving friend and neighbour, Lady Eleanor O'Flaherty.

She telephoned, Eleanor shouted cheerfully, 'Hey, what's this Mrs Caffrey tells me about Quill going walkabout, you —'

'Eleanor, don't —' Daisy gulped.

They talked, they cried, they gossiped, they asked each other unanswerable questions, finally, Eleanor had furiously scalding things to say about Edward. Daisy agreed with every one. Eleanor asked, 'Dear girl, you don't want me to get in touch with the bastard?'

'Why should you? I don't know where he is, anyway. Do you?'

'No. Devil a bit. Leave him to his own concerns, soon as he sniffs something for himself, he'll turn up. The shit.'

Since his visit by Quill, Hugh Stephenson had been in a state too critical to be questioned. Having now no friends, and Floy not in an emotional or physical state to visit, it was Daisy who sat by his bed, talked, randomly, of every Bankhill recollection she could dredge up, to no response. She felt so much alone, stranded with this dying man who was nothing to her but an unresponsive handclasp, a now reducing compendium of vanished memories.

Whenever she left, Sister Wainwright was there, a stoutly comforting arm round her waist, *you can't realise, Miss Donovan, how much this could mean to him…thank you for coming.*

Instead of giving way to tears, not for Hugh but for Quill, and Floy, and herself, she went out for a drink with Annette. 'I know I'm only third class,' Annette said. 'But what about making do with me while Mr Hunter's so tied up.'

'It's OK, I'm pretty quick on the uptake. Mixing with you lot *and* homilies from Floy about the difficulties of being a policeman's wife…'

Oh, God, are you really going to – do you mean? Marry? Hunter? Have I lost him forever? She must tell James. He'd go all knowing and superior and say of course Hunter wasn't going to let this one go, everyone, everyone knew he'd never been in such a state before.

It was necessary they talk about Hugh, there was sympathy between them but practicality, too, which Daisy understood. Annette asked, 'Can you remember, it could help, anything he said to you when you first visited him? When he could – I know it was limited – communicate.'

'Really, Annette, I don't think I've ever met the man before in my life. All right, I'd always known about him as a close friend of the Mannerings, he rambled about oh, so many things, people, from his past.'

'Yes. What did he say about Quill?'

'Well, he wanted to see him. He became rather – not upset – urgent. But I don't know how much was an old man's maunderings.'

'Never mind. Can you remember his words? Just take it easy, think back. Doesn't matter if they don't make sense. Where were you sitting? On a chair by his bed?'

'Yes, until I got up to go and then —'

'No,' Annette said gently, 'start at the beginning. You said hallo, sat down. Go through it again in sequence, you might find it helps you remember.'

Daisy told her how at first she'd mistaken his welcome for recognition of who she was, why she was there; then his obvious confusion, his lengthy ramblings interspersed with random demands to see Quill.

'Then he said – I can't remember why, perhaps for no reason – Clive's name. Edward's. Floy's, not necessarily in that order —'

Annette had taken out a pen and fished out of her handbag an envelope containing her gas bill and was busy making notes.

'Sink me,' Daisy said in her Sir Percy Blakeney voice.

'Look, I'm a copper. All right? Who is Edward?'

The look on Daisy's face indicated she was trying out various answers. 'Quill's lover.'

'OK,' Annette shrugged. And when Daisy volunteered nothing else, queried, 'Just what, exactly, is the connection to Hugh?'

'Who can say? I told you, Hugh's mind is all over the place. Edward is probably completely irrelevant.'

'Mm. Go on.'

'All right,' Daisy sighed. It seemed a long time ago, so much had happened in between, the two people concerned both dead. 'Something about Quill staying in Ireland to keep away from – something – sorry I can't dredge that up. Then he said, "Important." He'd kept it safe – whatever it was – with Floy, for Irene.'

'Who's Irene?'

Daisy explained, thought again: the clasp of his dry, hot hand, the sideways twist of his head. 'No, he said "her sister" not Irene's name. That was as I was leaving, and he got rather upset.'

After Daisy had gone back to keep Floy company, Annette and James wound up their weary day and went for supper at a favourite Thai restaurant. The only development that could scarcely rate as significant was the apprehension of the two youths surprised by the garage attendant in the act of stealing Quill's wallet. He had given a reasonable description of them which was recognised by more than one of the local uniformed force. Under-age, underprivileged, undersized, illiterate and neglected. As George Withers said, 'If I was in the same way as those two poor little bastards I'd rob dead bodies. There'd be not much else to do.' Their crime was opportunistic, apart from the unlikelihood of their being motivated or capable of murder, the forensic evidence established Quill had been killed several hours before they came upon his body at Cut End. They were drifting, scavenging, no one had been around, they could supply no useful information. They had taken his money, spent it, sold the credit cards outside a pub to someone they didn't know. Annette asked what Hunter was doing about them. James said, 'Nothing, let them off with a caution. The last thing we want in an on-going murder enquiry is stuff like that cluttering up space.'

They agreed between themselves that although he hadn't said anything directly, Hunter was punishing himself for not taking Quill's disappearance seriously. But then, what could he have done at the time? Annette told him about her talk with Daisy. 'Sometimes, I have a feeling, she's keeping things back.'

'What things?'

'How do I know? When you think, there's something about her – she has no ties, she doesn't belong, she's come from nowhere. Her only attachment seems to be to the Mannerings – well, what there's now left of them. Floy and Clive. But what do we know about her? There's this random element, existential.'

James was sceptical. 'I wouldn't dress it up as that. She hides family secrets, don't we all?'

'Yes. I wonder if she hides them from Hunter?'

'Perhaps that's her attraction, she's a woman of mystery,' James ventured.

'I'd say her attraction was pretty bloody obvious, even to you.'

'Yeah. If I was straight I'd fancy her.'

Media interest would have been more distressing to Floy if she had understood the extent of it. Everyone conspired to shield her from the vulgar tabloids: *Shock death of titled, fox-hunting gent – police appealing for information – mystery of his last lost hours –* and, in no time, inevitably, *handsome young live-in companion not yet traced.* Even reliable channels of information, the *Telegraph,* the radio, BBC2, trespassed upon her with their speculations; that was manageable, switch off, don't listen, don't read.

Grace had discreetly talked to neighbours, reporting to Daisy that scarcely had the news broken than the *Chatfield Argos* crew had appeared in Palmerston. To a outsider's view Floy was withdrawn but nevertheless doing what she did to perfection, behaving well. There was no sign of weeping, none of the distractions of grief. Only Daisy really knew how securely she was shut away inside herself, functioning like an automaton: punctilious and unfeeling. She made no decisions, politely attempted to do whatever anyone suggested. If Daisy did not sit her down at mealtimes, she was quite sure Floy would have stopped eating; as it was, most of her usual sparrow's portion was left on the plate.

Daisy spoke to her doctor, to Clive, to Grace – *she's in denial.* Yes, very well. She'd sit it out, wait for the floodgates to open.

But Floy's increasingly insubstantial look, her absence from self, left the uncanny impression that if only she could continue to hold herself in this suspended state she could go on behaving *as if nothing had happened.* For Daisy, the numbness of grief gave way to outbursts of infuriated bafflement – who would *do* such a dreadful, senseless thing?

When she asked Hunter he gave her all sorts of statistics from his world of the monstrously unpredictable, motiveless crime; she had a distant sense of adding to the burden of his everyday concerns, he had a murder to solve, personal, impersonal, why should she hamper him with her forlorn despair?

He said she should, he said, yell, shout, hit me if you like, curse everyone. Then he held her in his arms, was kind and passionate and for a while they forgot everything.

Hunter called Annette and Collier into his office, Mary Clegg was there. He said, 'Mary's done some pretty quick footwork. Go ahead.'

'It was George Withers put me onto it,' Mary said. She told them about the lock-up on Donkey Lane, the eye witness, the BMW.

Collier ventured, 'I don't suppose…'

'Reg? No, anyway, reg or not, she was too taken up with the driver. Over six feet, smartly dressed, fair-haired, good looking – a proper fella.'

Annette and James spoke together. 'Clive.'

They absorbed the information in silence for a moment, then Annette said, 'There's nothing we can do with this, is there, guv?'

'No, we'd never get a search warrant, we've no grounds, it could be anyone's BMW, without the registration number we can't connect it to anything.'

Collier asked, 'Do we know the owner of the lock-up?'

Mary said, 'He knows us, we put him away, possession of

stolen goods. His cousin's renting it, Nosey Skinner. Very nasty.'

Hunter was positive, 'If there is anything in this then we stay away from him, don't show our hand, don't let him know what we're thinking, just in case, if he's alerted, we could lose out.'

Annette said, 'That receptionist at the Manor – we didn't ask her for a description – why should we when he gave his name to her?'

'And he's made a statement to the fact that it wasn't him, he wasn't there, he was at home all evening. But no one can verify that,' Hunter added.

'And a BMW revving outside his house,' Mary said.

Hunter sighed, 'It's all circumstantial, and just not enough. All right, we keep looking at him closely. You'd better go back and see that receptionist, Annette, but first, let's see if we can get a photograph of him. If so, you can show it to your witness, Mary.'

Where was he going to get a photograph? He could scarcely ask Daisy, he was already vertiginously threatened by the Mannering's altitude when it came to reticence. He knew that, in spite of what Daisy was keeping from him, with patience and persistence, he'd eventually find out. And with his engulfing, protective love for her, how did he ask? *Will you lend me a photograph of your darling Clive so that someone can identify him as the possible murderer of Quill?*

Oh God.

He'd reckoned without the resourceful Annette. She had a friend on the *Chatfield Argos*, and remembering a prestigious event, with worthies drawn from business, charities, and local government, spun a story. The dear old Argos produced from its picture library a spitting image photograph of Clive awarding something to someone or congratulating someone on something.

Annette and Mary took copies of the photograph, went about their business. In both cases, the Manor receptionist and Annie looked closely for a long time, said, sorry, no, that's not the man. Almost, but not quite.

Hunter swore. Was it relief it wasn't Clive? Or a step back? Where the hell are we now?

Annette said, 'Look, guv, it's only a photo of his *face* – that doesn't take into account his build, height, the way he moves —'

Hunter said, 'Listen, I'll tell you what's been bothering me. This trail is too obvious. Someone announcing himself 'Clive Mannering'. Then the sighting of the BMW outside Clive's house; for good measure making one hell of a noise so it's bound to attract attention.'

'You mean someone setting him up?'

'The jig-saw syndrome: fitting evidence together to make up the picture we want to see – regardless of any relation to the facts. We don't make the evidence fit the crime, and I'm buggered if I'm going to let someone else do it for us.'

The next day, on receiving news that Hugh Stephenson had died, Hunter went to the Manor. His encounter with Sister Wainwright was difficult, but when it came to authority, the weight was all on his side. He told her it was important they search Mr Stephenson's room and he would like her permission.

'Mr Hunter, this isn't within my remit. I must ask —'

'Yes, I know. And time will depend on who you ask and how, we can do it the bureaucratic way, through time-consuming processes which will come between us and our job, or... Sir Aquilla died brutally, we are bound to investigate not only in the name of the law, but for the sake of his family. As far as we know the last person he spoke to was Mr Stephenson. There could be something, something here that could give us a lead. You can be present during our search, in fact, I'd prefer you to be.'

She hesitated for only a moment. 'Yes, yes. That won't be necessary, I'm sure your people are completely trustworthy.'

'Thank you. How was Mr Stephenson after Sir Aquilla saw him?'

'He was asleep. Sir Aquilla told me they talked a great deal, he stayed with Mr Stephenson till he went to sleep. I think he felt he wouldn't see him again – except of course, nobody could anticipate such a tragic outcome —' the admirable woman temporarily lost for words. It wouldn't happen often, Hunter thought.

Hunter tasked Annette and DC Barlow to search his room. Barlow had shown himself alert and intuitive. Annette was attuned, by proxy, to the rhythms and realties of Bankhill life as exemplified by Hugh Stephenson.

They went quietly about their work, respectful of the life and death of a human being contained in the beautiful room. Nothing significant occurred, his more complicated legal concerns were not their business. Eventually Barlow said quietly, 'Nothing here, is there? Shall we wrap up?'

'I suppose so,' Annette said. She was sitting on the chair she knew Daisy had sat on, holding the hand of a dying man, looking at the superb photographs, the arc of Hugh's life.

She studied each one of the portraits, so eloquent, so perfectly framed and presented. Those two boys, Clive and who? Their wild youth contained in the conventions of the time: school uniform, short haircuts, scrubbed look. Sir Aquilla – what a pitiable end for that elegant, courtly man.

She imagined Daisy sitting there on that first occasion, when Hugh had been able to speak, tugging at her wrist in his urgency to see Quill. Names: Clive, Edward, Floy. The sister? Whose sister? Something he'd kept safe, for Floy? No – *it's there with Floy*.

Floy, then an exquisite young woman, dignified, vulnerable: sensitive of him to place her in the dining room, exemplifying the shelter of Fairmead, the calm reaches of her life.

And that one portrait – Annette's gaze moved scrupulously, assessing. Just this one was minutely mis-aligned, a fraction out of true within its frame. If she hadn't been looking so intently she would have missed it. She reached forward.

DC Barlow said, 'What is it, Annette?'

Then he saw she was concentrating, working silently, went to stand beside her as she removed the backing from the photograph. And there, behind one photograph, another.

Puzzling.

A monochrome photograph of a woman lying on a pavement beside a bicycle. The dark stain on the pavement's edge by her head. A boy in shorts, balancing his bicycle, staring down at her.

So young. So unmistakable. Clive.

Chapter Twenty-Five

Annette and Hunter talked about it exhaustively, he had, through Daisy, a mosaic of family history. There had been Irene's late marriage, early and unexpected death, an accident – he knew no more than that. Annette could supplement information, she had inherited the social sweep – what one did, accepted, talked about, didn't mention. 'You don't know anything about it, I suppose.'

She shook her head. 'I can ask my mum, she might. I'll phone her this evening.'

'You could do it now.'

'Sorry, day out with the WI, God knows where they'll be.' She hesitated, this was personal, but there were times when the job came first. 'You could ask Daisy.'

'I could.' As he spoke she began to search through her handbag, he assumed as a polite way of diverting him from embarrassment. 'But if Daisy thinks there are private places in the Mannerings' lives, she won't tell me. And I don't want to open up old wounds for Floy, she's only just coping as it is.'

'Yes, of course. Ah, here it is.' She drew out an envelope. 'When I talked to Daisy about the first time she visited Hugh at the Manor, I wrote down what she could remember.'

He could always rely on her. None of it might matter, but some whisper told him it *could*.

She read through her notes, the few words, the names. 'I suppose they were people he was close to at one time, still felt he was, they were on his mind. Clive. Quill. Edward,' she hesitated. 'According to Daisy, Quill's boyfriend.'

'I had worked that out for myself. Daisy can't stand him, she doesn't like to talk about him.'

'And Irene. She was Floy's sister and she died suddenly, in an accident.'

'And Hugh was keeping something important with Floy for Irene.'

'This?'

Later on, he sought her out. 'I have to speak to Clive. I'm not going to take you with me. You understand. You're too close to us, Daisy and me.'

Something had worn into Clive: grief? Uncertainty? His hair was ruffled, his face drawn.

'Sheldon —' an automatically warm greeting – his gaze passing to Mary Clegg, in her plain civvies. His 'Good evening, Miss Clegg,' was answered by a nod, not the informality of 'Call me Mary.' Efficient, controlled, they stepped in to Clive's fashionable territory. He offered them a drink. They declined. '*Is this official?*'

Is this official? Daisy asked when he had connived, deliberately cornered her in the Blue Piano. *Is this official?*

They sat facing across a low glass table, Hunter and Mary on one side, Clive on the other. Hunter thought of him the first time he had seen him at Fairmead, the blazer and flannels, the confident charm; and then his courtesy at Floy's dinner party, the high spirits he shared with Daisy. Wordlessly, he produced the photograph, placed it in front of Clive.

His reaction was instantaneous, he sat back, turned his head away, then looked at Hunter in disbelief and amazement 'Who had it?'

It was the last thing Hunter expected him to say. He answered impassively, 'Who do you think?'

Still looking anywhere except at the photograph, he spoke as if asking himself a long, stubborn question. 'Not Quill?'

'You're not denying it's you?' Hunter said. 'No, of course not, it was how long ago?'

'Nineteen fifty-nine.'

'But you're plainly identifiable. And you know who the lady is, don't you?'

He pulled himself up, with an air of pain, nodded. 'Mrs Crane. Miss Mannering's sister Irene. Where *did* you get this?'

'The best thing at the moment, Clive, is you explain the circumstances when and why it was taken. Then I'll tell you.'

A pause, the intimation of a man delving memories; Hunter knew only too well the missed chances of allowing time. He leaned forward, 'Clive?'

'I was with Edward – Edward Crane, Mrs Crane was his stepmother – we were cycling around Bankhill. We suddenly came on her, lying on the road. We'd both had birthdays, his present was a Kodak camera. I stopped to look down at her – he photographed me. Then we – we saw we couldn't do anything and we rode off. We – we were afraid to tell anyone in case we were blamed.'

As he said nothing else, Mary asked, 'Why should you be?'

'There was a game played that summer…' He explained what it was, that they had never dared, there had been talk about it going too far, and punishments; one lady had suffered a broken arm, with consequent utter disgrace, not only for the boy but for his irreproachable family. They decided to keep quiet, cycle away as quickly as possible. There were never any questions asked, if there had been, if anyone had seen them, they would have been able honestly to say they spent the afternoon cycling to Alderley Edge and back. 'Now, will you tell me,' he asked quietly.

Mary wondered whether the brief account was something he had never spoken of from that time to this. She was not sure it was accurate.

Hunter said, 'Hugh Stephenson,' read the *of course, who else?* on Clive's face. 'Can you tell me why it should be in his possession?'

'Well, you know he was a professional photographer. He was very keen to encourage youngsters to use cameras, he ran the youth camera club.'

They waited. He looked down, not at the photograph on the table, but at his cared-for, manicured hands, clasped tightly. Hunter said, 'Do you expect us to accept that as an explanation?'

Clive murmured, 'I don't know what else I can say.'

'He ran the youth camera club. A group activity I presume? And you both – what? – turned up at a meeting and asked him to develop the film. A lady whose death would have been local talk, who was related to —'

'Oh, I see what you mean. No, of course, it wasn't like that. Hugh was very friendly with Uncle Quill, that was how I knew him, and Edward was my friend and particularly keen on photography. So,

Hugh let us use his studio to play around in, experiment with various techniques. As a matter of fact, I didn't know at the time that Edward had taken that photo – everything was so, so sudden. He developed that, I didn't know he had, and – Hugh found it, he showed it to me, then he confiscated it. I give you my word, Sheldon, I never knew it still existed, I haven't set eyes on it since then. And I'd have known if anyone else ever saw it.'

'By "anyone" you mean who? Quill? Did he know of it? Had he seen it?'

'I don't know, he and Hugh were so close, and Edward and I were involved... They wouldn't have wanted it broadcast. He could have seen it, but obviously, they'd both keep it quiet.'

Mary said, 'Mr Mannering, you said earlier that there were never any questions asked after Mrs Crane's death. There was no investigation?'

'You mean police and inquest and so on? No, nothing like that. Official enquiries, obviously, it was found she was in the early stages of glaucoma, this could cause giddiness, disorientation. And as it transpired, she'd been having spells – falling down. There was nothing to link us with the incident, no one knew we'd – found her. In fact, immediately afterwards I went on holiday with my parents to our cottage in Devon. My brother and I stayed there with my mother for the rest of the summer. My father came back to Chatfield after a fortnight, but the funeral was over by then. My parents liked Mr Crane but they never, well, they didn't have a lot in common with him —'

And Mr Crane had been married to a Skinner, and a Skinner funeral was something to avoid. Of course, Hunter would not say this; he gauged how the inconsequential conversation relaxed Clive. He gave Mary the merest nod.

'Mr Mannering, you remember when DC Barlow and I spoke to you on the day Sir Aquilla's body was found.'

'Of course. You took a statement from me.'

'Yes. You said you hadn't seen Sir Aquilla for over two years.'

He looked lost. 'Did I? Well, yes?'

Hunter said, 'You'd been out of touch for all that time?'

'What? Oh, I see. No, not completely, we spoke on the phone

every so often, sent the occasional card.'

Hunter said in an everyday voice, 'Just chat, family matters.'

Mary said, 'He didn't tell you he'd changed his car to a BMW?'

Clive said neutrally, 'He might. If he did, it slipped my mind.'

After the merest pause, Hunter observed with mild interest that one of the photographs in Hugh's room was of Clive and another boy. That would be Edward?

Clive, momentarily disconcerted, nodded, then pre-empting Hunter's next question, 'We lost touch, oh, years ago. Schooldays over and that sort of thing.' His eyes now on the photograph, he asked in a diffident, awkward way, 'Um, what will you do with – um.'

Hunter let him flounder for a moment, interested in his manner. At no time had he presumed on his association with Hunter through Daisy; this was an unmistakable personal note. 'Legally, of course, it's part of Mr Stephenson's estate and, eventually, it'll go to whoever inherits.' He paused. Clive said nothing, his expression closed. He was an intelligent man, he knew Hunter had more to say, he waited. Hunter found this interesting. 'For the present, though, we need to hang on to it.'

Clive nodded, his relief incompletely concealed. He didn't claim it as his own property, question why they should hold on to it. Hunter glanced towards Mary.

She said, 'So, aside from Mr Stephenson and, you assume, possibly Sir Aquilla, who else might have seen this? Mr Crane, Irene's husband?'

He shook his head firmly, 'I'm sure not. Why would anyone show it to the man? He had enough grief to cope with.'

'Who indeed?' Hunter mused.

Mary asked, 'Do you think Miss Mannering —'

'Absolutely not. It was in Hugh's keeping, he would never, never... No.'

But, and the reality hung heavily unspoken; he had kept it all these years, concealed it. A time bomb waiting to go off.

On the drive back to Talbot Way, Mary said, 'He certainly didn't press us to hand that photo over to him, to anyone, did he?'

'No, we'll hang on to it, just in case. It couldn't be anywhere safer than in our custody, could it? He's a respectable and respected man, he'd hardly want that circulating.' Especially amongst the Skinners, if they got their hands on it the opportunity for blackmail... As they were leaving, he said diffidently, 'There's no need for Daisy to know about this. She's upset enough about Quill.'

'Thank you, Sheldon.' Clive would never have asked, but his voice cracked with relief.

Mary was speaking. He said, 'Sorry, I was just following a thought. What?'

'At the time it happened, Hugh Stephenson, Sir Aquilla...two men with those two boys. They could have had pretty good reason to keep quiet, apart from that photo.'

'Yes. Eleven-year-olds.' And Quill, the adored *verray parfit gentil knight*. The boys such disparate types, thrown together by unexpected connection. Clive, gentleman-in-the-making, with his gullibility and naïvety. Edward – Hunter was imprinted with the same life pattern, knew, from the first time he ever went out without his mother, about street fighting and survival. And these two boys had one golden afternoon witnessed the death of an elderly woman connected to them both. And lied about it. And two greatly respected gentlemen who had colluded with them were now dead.

There was some fall-out from this. There had to be.

With no other justification than that he was obeying the strictures of professionalism, Hunter kept his word and told Daisy nothing about Clive and the photograph. But the conjunction of that apparent accident with the present, as if the action had not been completed and the players were reassembled on the stage: Quill. Clive. Irene. Edward...

Quill's inquest had opened and adjourned, pending criminal proceedings; Clive was paying a quick visit to Ireland assisting with the funeral arrangements. Daisy stayed with Floy. Hunter took her out to dinner that evening and later, at his flat, when they were curled up together, he said, 'Daisy, I need to talk to you about Quill. You understand anything you can tell me, the smallest, least significant detail, could lead us somewhere important.'

They talked over wearingly covered ground, then she hesitated. He studied her expressive face. 'I'd quite forgotten, Sheldon, because I don't suppose it means anything —' she told him about the telephone call Mrs Lowe had taken on the morning they expected Quill. 'But he didn't give his name, and she didn't recognise the voice.'

No. But someone had taken the trouble to check up he would be arriving that day, and the time. Who wanted to know, and why?

'But when Quill was —' she drew breath, steadied her voice, 'when he was murdered, Floy and I were waiting for him, together —'

'No, darling, that's not what I mean, it's nothing as specific as that. Just talk.'

'About what?' her helpless exasperation.

'All right, all right. Quill and Hugh, when they were younger and Clive and Edward were boys. No, I know you were only occasionally around then – but since, has there been any hint about the kind of relationship these men had with them?'

'Hint? Edward's been a tart all his life. As for Clive, he knew he was gay when he was very young – twelve, thirteen – quite probably it was Edward helped him find out. I just assume that everyone talked about them being such chums, inseparable, so, they had pleasure, they used each other – Edward was an expert at that. Sheldon, you're the one who lives in the real world, you know that boys —'

'Yes, of course, but that's not what I asked. I meant —'

'All right, I'm getting round to that.' With reluctance, by the sound of her voice. He stroked her hair, she relaxed against him.

'I'm sorry, forgive me. I didn't mean to snap. It's just that, Quill and Hugh are both dead now, and there's something hurtful about... Well, the truth is, I don't know what went on all that time ago. Certainly no one ever said anything that I heard. You know, there was a great innocence then, everyone knew and didn't say, if you see what I mean. I don't believe anyone was damaged or corrupted – if you ask me, it was the other way round where Edward's concerned, he's quite capable of seducing anyone. Later on he became a fixture, more or less, in Quill's life. He's lived with him in Ireland, well, sometimes, for at least the last ten years.'

'When did you last see him?'

'Two years ago, in Ireland, hunting holiday,' her tone grew hesitant. 'It was obvious the relationship was under strain, after that it was on and then off, it might even be quite over.'

'What makes you think that?'

She answered there had always been dramas, then explained that as far as she knew, whenever Quill came to visit Edward came too, but never appeared at Fairmead. 'Floy just won't have him, I suppose he goes off to his ghastly family, they idolise him. Naturally, their very own home-grown con artist.'

He had heard Daisy be rude about people before, often hilariously; there was no softening amusement in a voice where scorn and anger echoed.

'But this time, Quill came alone, and according to Mrs Caffrey, Edward went off somewhere several days ago. But he phoned, regularly, and the day we expected Quill, he was very rude to Mrs Caffrey. She's a dear woman, she was so upset.'

Hunter thought to ask if she thought this could have any bearing on events, but listening to her account of who had said what and with what outcome, was aware of her despairing guardianship of Mannering private business, about that, he could never doubt her shining honesty.

Chapter Twenty-Six

Shopping in Waitrose, Daisy found herself next to Big John. He took her hand, wordlessly, then put his arms round her, the unselfconscious decency of a man who would never be embarrassed by grief.

'Come on, let's talk.' It was no surprise to her he knew of the hidden herbalist. They sat behind their long glasses of hot sarsaparilla, 'You were fond of him. I never knew him personally, but always heard what a gentleman he was.'

'Oh yes…' Daisy talked, wandering through the solace of recollection. And then, 'It's odd, all that stuff Josie gave me, Clive passed it on to me, I've been reading Mrs Twemlow's diary, well journal —'

'Oh, sorry. Listen, if you'd just rather I appeared with a bin bag and absent-mindedly —'

'Hey, no, there's some really, well, interesting – and odd —'

He groaned, 'You mean Morris dancing and the poor children's picnic. You don't have to —'

'Poor children's – you've made that up.'

'No. My grandpa went on it, with his seven brothers. His mum cleaned lavatories in offices, she took the kids with her, to help her out. The picnic was once a year in Gortway Park. The kids ate till they burst, took home all the leftovers and were all given a pair of shoes.'

She gave him a sideways look, his comfortable acceptance of a world that had hammered out a tough generation, a world she had never known.

'Hell, that's put me in my place.'

'Come on. What was odd?'

'Oh, it just caught my attention. I admit I only glanced at it, something about Irene Mannering's – Crane's accident. It happened on Balmoral Drive.'

'Really? Josie's never said anything about it, but then, there'd be no – reason.' He had so obviously substituted 'reason' for 'interest'. 'D'you mean she saw it happen?'

'Oh, no – at least, I don't think so. I was only skimming

through, I think I'd have taken that in.' But who cared? What did it matter anymore? 'It was just funny, that I should have been reading that about the Mannerings, and now...'

The day was so dismal it seemed that autumn had been elbowed aside while winter, losing its place in the sequence of seasons, rushed through. Rain poured from dark skies, thunder banged, off-stage. By afternoon lights and heating were on at Fairmead; Floy had visitors to engage her in Earl Grey tea and scones and comfortingly inconsequential talk. Daisy seized every chance, and invented several, to juxtapose friends and food in the hope that Floy would be too interested to notice she was eating something. She took a phone call from Grace, who called every day or dropped in to see Floy, never intruding, always strengthening. She had an invitation Daisy conveyed to Floy, 'Would like you to have supper with Grace, just the two of you, this evening?'

Floy looked doubtful. 'Well, I... What about you?'

'Oh, I'll be fine, perhaps go out, don't know yet. If Sheldon's – um available.'

'He is most awfully busy, I know,' Floy said.

It was a precipice moment, no one could possibly say he was busy trying to find her cousin's murderer. Daisy agreed brightly and went back to the phone. 'She'd love to come, about sevenish?'

'Sure? If she changes her mind I'll quite understand.'

'I'm sure it'll be all right. She says yes to almost anything at present. I think she's just relieved to have someone make decisions for her.'

After her solitary supper, Daisy took herself into the garden room with a glass of wine and the armload of notebooks and scrapbooks and odds and ends that were Mrs Twemlowe's life. The rain had stopped, the light was little more than a dull glimmer, like green gauze, sweeping over the flattened flowers and broken foliage of drenched gardens.

She sorted through the folders, found what Mrs Twemlowe had called, in her touchingly old-fashioned term, her Everyday Books.

They were not conventional printed diaries, but bound journals with lined pages, she dated the entries whenever she had something to record, the years were printed on the spines. Daisy found the one she had glanced at before for nineteen fifty-nine, identifying it by its cover. A hunting scene. As a young woman Phyllis Twemlowe had been a fearless horsewoman – Quill had once told Daisy – riding side saddle and wearing violets on her lapel.

She turned up the entry for Wednesday 11th July.

I wrote up the minutes of the Floral Society this morning and this afternoon popped out with them across the road to Marjorie for her to type out and circulate. Just as I came out of our gate this lady was going past on a bicycle and after I'd popped over the road and was letting myself in at Marjorie's gate, two boys came along on bicycles.

I put the envelope into Marjorie's door, it was only seconds, not even minutes, and went back up her drive and looked along the road and there was the lady, lying on the pavement! I ran there – her head was on the kerb – there was a lot of blood – but she was still breathing. The road was absolutely deserted. I ran straight into Professor Cope's to ask her to phone for an ambulance. Well, I knew she'd be lecturing at the University but her cleaner was there, I'd seen her going in shortly after lunch. She didn't answer the door, though, so I ran back and Mrs Fanshawe and her old father had come out of their house. She went straightaway to phone and I sat down on the pavement. I saw then it was Irene Mannering – well, Crane now, I didn't know her very well. I just held her hand, poor lady, there was nothing else I could do, just talk to her. And then I realised she'd died, while I was talking to her, I don't know if she'd known I was there. I hope so. The ambulance came just then and I was surprised how many people had gathered around. Mrs Fanshawe's old father was regimenting them all – comes of having been in the army, I suppose, but no one could really do anything.

You don't think, it's always so quiet round here, and – safe, you don't think someone could die in the road. And it seemed so wrong somehow, we stood around talking about it, nobody could understand how it had happened, it wasn't as if there was an obstacle in the road, or oil to skid on or some speeding car.

Sunday 15th July
I wrote a letter of condolence to Floy Mannering. She hasn't replied yet, poor thing will be devastated, and she wasn't at church this morning. But then no one expected her, she and her sister were so close. It seems Irene had only been married five minutes, everyone said how happy she'd been with this Mr Crane and it's tragic for him because his first wife died only a couple of years ago, I believe.

I've been thinking and thinking about that afternoon, just an ordinary suburban road one summer afternoon, and no one there except those two boys, but they were cycling behind her. And then I thought later I might have imagined them, it was so bewildering, like an awful dream – everywhere was absolutely deserted seconds after it happened, no sign of the boys, no sign of anyone – although there was no mention of them later – it was as if they hadn't existed. Because if they had, this has been the talk of the neighbourhood, they'd have come forward wouldn't they? Said they'd seen her or not, but must have done, she was just in front of them. I tried to recall what they were like, did wonder for a minute if they could have been errand boys, well, most of us have our groceries and meat delivered, but errand boys have those heavy bikes, with baskets, and they dress differently. These boys were well dressed, one of them had something slung on his back, perhaps a camera, or binoculars, and their bikes would have been expensive, yes, I remember how the spokes sparkled, shining, catching the sun.

The police came and took measurements and asked people what they'd seen, I was the only one who'd seen anything – and I hadn't really, anyway. There's usually comings and goings round the Quadrant but being Wednesday afternoon all the shops were shut, Mr Ellis-Rowe was posting a letter and thought he saw her but he couldn't be sure and anyway, that's ten minutes from here, so it didn't help.

Tuesday 17th July.
Mrs Crane's funeral this morning. I didn't go, but Vera Barker did.
She said Grace Wilmot was there, with Floy, she'd bound to be, being
next door neighbours so long and having always known Irene. Some
more of the family were there, not Clive and his parents, they'll all be
at their cottage in Devon. Irene was so fond of him. Mr Crane with
his family, Vera said they were a nice, quiet lot, and Mr Crane's son,
don't know his name, was there, of course, Irene being his stepmother,
and, according to Vera, his family were a different matter entirely.
Very common and loud, she said, and I suppose she's right, she usually
is, having done a lot of voluntary work with deprived people, but I
can't help feeling for that boy, first his mother, then his stepmother, all
in two years. It's a lot for a youngster to stand up to.

Daisy sat still for a long time, the innocent, kind lady's record of
an unaccountable death unravelling inside her head, waiting for
understanding to catch up. A connection. She went to the study
for pencil and paper, sat down and read through again, scribbling
notes on the pad, underlining phrases here and there.

Balmoral Drive. And the house where Edward's Grandma
cleaned. Big John saying how proud she was to work for the lady
professor. And Mrs Twemlowe knew the professor's cleaner was
in but hadn't opened the door…

There was a truth ambushed there, a cataclysmic event
meshing mundane matters, undisclosed because Mrs Twemlowe
did not consider it important.

The long case clock chimed its reassuring, mellow notes. Grace
would walk Floy home later. The light was murky, but at least the
streets were refreshed, washed clean of dust, an evening walk
would be pleasant.

Chapter Twenty-Seven

On Balmoral Drive there were few steeply pitched roofs and sweeping gables, it had always had a certain edge, architecturally shaking off the Arts and Crafts, the Jacobean and thrusting itself into the future of the geometrically exact Moderne house with its flat roof, spare lines, suntrap windows.

More times than she could remember Daisy had walked, run, driven and cycled up Balmoral Drive and not absorbed the significance. Why should she? She had been far too young to know Irene; running through dates she worked out she'd been in Ireland with her mother at the time of Irene's death (had her mother attended the funeral?). Her first recollected visit to Fairmead had been almost two years later.

Ignoring the chill in the air, she lingered past the Twemlowe's house, glanced across the road to Marjorie's, Marjorie who would type the minutes of the Floral Society. Ahead, the insensible curve of the road, where Irene cycled, followed by two boys on bicycles.

She tried to replay the event in her mind's eye, but it was impossible. Time had moved on, the circumstance eluded her. There was only one way she could attempt to reconnect with the past – by the verification of people who had in some way participated in it.

She didn't ask herself why the truth of that day had suddenly become imperative, perhaps Quill's terrible death weighed on her, the dislocation of all the links – she just unthinkingly acted.

Returning briskly to Fairmead, she collected the car keys and got into the Mini. As she drove away, the last of the daylight gave her the diminishing view through her mirror of the enclosing foliage, the abundant gardens of Palmerston Avenue.

Although the houses on the Easton estate were identical, she had no trouble finding the one Big John had pointed out to her, the corner house with its garden of strict, ferociously ordered vegetables.

The thin door knocker made an irritable rapping sound. She

stood back. No porch shielded her unwelcome presence from the Grandparents; they would have heard her car draw up, anyway. The merest flicker of alteration in light as the front window curtain twitched, resettled. She waited. There was nothing she could do if they refused to open the door, she couldn't bang on windows, shout through the letter box. The confused determination that had carried her there had settled to a bludgeoned sense of purpose, she would find out, she would know.

From behind the closed door, sounds as stealthy as mice, then the scraping of bolts, the rattle of unfastening chains.

Grandmother confronted her, every angle of her small body taut with rejection. Behind her, a little further down the hall, Grandfather. The house was a duplicate of Brenda's; narrow, but free of clutter; the light was meagre, there was a greyness of carpet and décor, the greyness of two old, expressionless faces.

She was surprised at her own composure. 'I would very much like to speak to you both, if you could spare a few moments.'

'You would, would you? And what would that be about?'

Treacherously, her heart lurched. She spoke slowly, keeping her voice steady. 'It's about the day Irene – Mrs Crane – died. On Balmoral Drive. You were working there that day.'

She had said it all. Beyond that was the disturbing sense of their lack of surprise. The old lady looked beyond her, an unnervingly busying look, as if there was someone more important and interesting standing on the narrow path behind her; she almost turned to make sure, stopped herself. Then Mrs Skinner turned and gazed back at her husband. 'Let her in,' he snapped.

Grandmother sat on a straight-backed chair at a table, Grandfather stood with his back to the fireplace and old-fashioned unlit gas fire. She was not asked to sit down, stood under a glaring centre light in a room of uncompromising neatness. Every flat surface was crammed with ornaments, a skimming glance revealed them as souvenirs, family gifts ranging decades and the world, from Blackpool to Lanzarotte. The worn, polished furniture was adorned with crocheted covers in every colour and pattern of wool. Just for an instant there was a distracting scent of something expensive, untraceable, exotic in the drab surroundings.

Grandmother spoke to her but, disconcertingly, looked at her husband. 'Well, go on, spit it out.'

She was at once calm, everything lined up in her head, arguments, explanations, questions.

She began, 'On that day, a Wednesday the ninth of July —'

'History lesson, is it?' the old man barked at his wife. It seemed they were prepared to speak at her but only by deflecting their comments off each other, as if by ignoring her presence they could render her invisible.

She hung on to a grim politeness. 'You'll remember the day, won't you?' she said to Grandmother. 'It was one of your days for cleaning at Professor Cope's.'

Again a disconcerting lack of surprise. A sly triumph, 'You trying to accuse me of something?'

Not even trying to make sense of this, Daisy persevered. 'It was normally such a quiet road – but that day, after Irene's accident, Mrs Twemlow knocked at Professor Cope's door but you didn't answer – and there were people knocking on other doors, neighbours gathered, wanting to help, voices, then an ambulance, directly outside the house. You must have been aware —'

'I'd me work to do. I'd not be bothering what was going on, not with any tittle-tattle or whatever.' This was rapped out with all the stridency of the self-righteous, supplemented by an approving grunt from Grandfather.

'Tittle...' Daisy struggled with the belittlement of a life and death situation. 'This was a woman you knew – she was your grandson's stepmother. You must have seen   '

'I didn't see nothing. You've never had to work for your living, young woman. You don't go looking out windows and leaving things, just leaving things, to stand about gossiping and gawping.'

'Mrs Skinner, people were trying to help Irene, they weren't —' the word stuck in her throat, so judgmental, so dismissive, 'they weren't gawping.'

'That sort, round there, they've nothing else to do. They don't have to earn their own livings. Just posh, idle, order other folks about.'

'You were there, that day, in Professor Cope's house. You saw, didn't you – from the window? You saw Irene cycle past, then she was followed by two boys on bicycles. Did you see them? Did you know who they were?'

Two set faces stared at each other. Whatever they communicated, she was excluded.

'You'd worked for the professor for a long time, you must have known so many people by sight. Mrs Twemlowe said —'

An outburst of naked spite, 'Mrs Twemlowe, Mrs Twemlowe – she's not saying nothing to nobody. She's gone ga-ga. How would you know what-Mrs-Twemlowe-said,' Grandmother taunted, singsong voice, waggling head – a scaldingly shaming replay of the scene in the kitchen at Canal Road.

Grandfather gave a derisive bark that could have been a laugh, although there was no amusement in it. 'You go taking notice of *Mrs Twemlowe* and you'll make a right fool of yourself.'

Daisy waited for embarrassment and distaste to reduce before answering firmly, 'Because I've read her diary.' A wall of incomprehension. How would they ever have had time to keep diaries, even the inclination was unlikely.

She explained carefully how Mrs Twemlowe had written down into a notebook all the events of her life, large and small. And, most importantly, the entry for the day Irene died – and afterwards. 'She saw Irene lying on the pavement and she ran and knocked at Professor Cope's door because she knew you were there and she wanted you to phone for an ambulance. But you didn't answer, did you?'

The two old people stared at each other, expressionless, mute.

She tried again, patient, with genuine interest, asking, 'Why didn't you?' just as fruitlessly. Then, 'Afterwards the police made enquiries. Did they ask you? No, I don't suppose so, they didn't know you were there, might even have seen —'

Grandfather shouted, making her jump, 'You want to be careful what you go around saying.'

'I'm not saying anything —'

'You go around slandering people – there's the lore,' he shouted.

'Dad —' Grandmother made a gesture that could have meant anything, spared Daisy an accusatory sideways glance.

He continued, volume reduced, trembling before another upsurge, 'Think because you're being a slut with that high-up policemen you can go round slandering people. Well, you can't get away with it, get him into trouble you will, he'd be disciplined, yes, disciplined, on account of you.' He nodded, with enormous satisfaction, Grandmother was nodding, too, measured this time, in affirmation.

Daisy said steadily, 'I've no idea what you're talking about —'

The atmosphere had become unbreathably dense, they were neither of them listening to her. Grandfather's spleen erupted, beginning with garbled accusations of her putting our John's children in danger and then, loud, excited, jabbing his finger at her, 'There's all that sodding money that should have come to our Edward from his father.' He was growing increasingly coarse, and enjoying it, face reddened, eyes staring.

'Language, Dad,' Grandmother warned, shrill.

'What money?' Daisy faltered.

'What money, what money?' Grandmother's singsong voice, waggling head. Then, 'You Mannerings, all of you, take the lot.'

'For heaven's sake,' Daisy fumbled through appalling inessentials. 'Are you talking about – it was Irene's money, not Stanley's.'

'They were man and wife, what was hers was his,' Grandfather was yelling. 'You can't do nothing about mother being there when that stuck-up bitch died. Nothing. You think you can tell your *boyfriend*? You daren't…' his seamed face, rheumy eyes, the blast of stale onion breath as he thrust close, 'Because there's the photo.'

'Photo?'

'Oh, yes. One with that disgusting nancy – your Clive – standing over her ladyship Irene's body lying on road next to her bike —'

What else did he say? A jumble of condemnation, blame, '— Mother'd not shop her own.'

'What?'

The old lady's liver-spotted claw on his, 'You'd best not say nothing else —'

He shook her off. This was his triumph, someone at last was meeting a long overdue reckoning. 'Our Edward's been having that Hugh whatsit watched, by people as he can trust. Not you swindling lot. He wasn't going to have that photo passed on somewhere else, do us out of our proof.'

'Photo?' she said again, helplessly, trying to find her place in a landslip.

There was more, confusingly, somewhere amongst it, Quill's guilt – and Hugh's – for leading Edward astray, abusing him —

'D'you know they did that to our Edward? Do you? Polluted him, they did, a motherless lad, an orphan, helpless, innocent. And I'll tell you what, Sir Ack-what, got what was coming to him. Some victim of his saw him off, waited their chance and saw him off, and good riddance.'

There was some kind of defence, if only she could find her voice. Edward had been living off Quill for years, betraying him, swindling him, smirching his dignity; if she tried to say that they would shout her down. She had been part of Quill's plenteous life as they never had – the only thing she could think with some coherence – whatever Quill had got out of his relationship with Edward – had it been worth it to him?

Grandfather was shouting again with a vigour that clacked his false teeth, jabbing his finger at her in incomprehensible accusation. Grandmother was staring straight at her; nodding, her button eyes glinting with triumph, her voice pattering about beneath his, '— he'll have an attack – fatal, could – all your fault —'

She stood speechless at the mercy of their hatred as random particles of understanding gathered, cohered. She had done no good here. She couldn't think, for a moment, why she had come at all.

She went out by herself, the ragged voice following her, left the house with its smell of old bodies and striving and lovelessness.

* * *

In the abrupt fold of silence the door to the kitchen opened. They turned, Grandfather said, 'You heard?'

'Yes. Just – forget about this. Say nothing. You understand.'

'Will she go to that policeman? Filth. Her fancy man?'

'No, I'll see she doesn't. Go to bed. I don't think anyone'll knock, if they do, don't answer the door. When I get back, I'll tell you what to say.'

They nodded. They would silently acknowledge to each other that ever since he had begun the transition from discarded, meaningless boy to powerful maturity, they had always done as he said...

In the deepened dusk, Daisy crumpled against the Mini with the hurt of the past, of present cruelties. She found she was crying; fished for her handkerchief, then the car keys.

'Daisy, we have to talk —'

She gasped, spun round. The sudden, other presence, the level, concerned voice. And in a glance of street light Edward's face, so handsome, so sympathetic.

His hand came forward, a calming gesture. 'All right, Daisy, we've had our fallings out, but...we've both had a bereavement, our darling Quill, I know how much he meant to you. They can never know, you mustn't blame them, their ignorance —'

'What?' She was wiping away her betraying tears, fumbling for car keys, and he was talking in his beautifully languid voice. 'Come along.' His actions firm, quietly decisive, seeing her into the car, going swiftly round the bonnet, getting in beside her.

'Start up, we haven't got much time, I'll explain as we go.'

'Where?' she was slow, carrying the burden of an ingrained hatred and rage she couldn't begin to understand.

He gave her directions, she followed them because it was something to do, not think about, get away.

'You need to know why they said that terrible thing about Clive. It's not true, of course, but it's something they've believed for years, it's all very complicated —'

'Edward, how do you know what they said – about Clive?'

'Because they were talking about it earlier, it's an obsession with them. I came in by the back door, more or less as you were leaving; I only needed to hear a few words – Grandpa was shouting, after all – and I knew what they must have been saying to you. They've been harbouring this – resentment so long they can't let go of it. They – wrongly, blame so much on the Mannerings, and that includes you. I promise, I'll explain everything —'

He directed her through the roads she knew, where she was at home, and safe. Short way down the bypass, then the Quadrant, past the foliaged turn into Balmoral, Railway Road.

'Pull up here. OK, we can walk. Come on.' He was brisk, at once round to her side, opening the door for her.

'What…'

'Hurry up, we don't want to be too late for him.' He was striding on, lithe, light. She could match his pace without trouble, tugged along by uncomprehending urgency.

'Who?'

'Clive,' he said, as if she should know; when she slowed in surprise, he took her arm, hurried with her along the tunnel of shrubs that formed the walk leading towards the track. 'He wants to tell you, he needs to tell you. He needs your help.'

They were almost running. 'Edward, I don't —'

'Ssh, we must keep quiet. He knows he can rely on you. "Daisy'll help, she'd never let me down," he said to me.'

'What did you mean – *too late*? What are you trying to —'

'Oh, Daisy, it's so hard for him —' His indistinct words weaving in and out of the sound of their footsteps, his face so intent – then suddenly they paused and he moved a barrier and she realised where they were: on the old footbridge. 'Where…?' She looked for Clive. And with the sudden closeness of Edward's presence, that exotic, expensive scent. Aftershave. 'Edward – you were there, weren't you – in your grandparents' house —'

The railway lines beneath her, silver in the moonlight: past – present – future. She thought, inconsequential comfort, Far Twittering to Oyster Creek…standing there, with Sheldon, his strength, his arms around her…

Chapter Twenty-Eight

Daisy had left the hall lights on for her, of course she would, always so conscientious, and walking along Grace's path, Floy had glimpsed through the bushes the oblong of light from the garden room painted on the lawn.

But when she went in there she found it empty, she pottered about, kitchen, dining room, 'Daisy, are you in, darling?' No, of course not, delayed recognition – the Mini was not in the drive. Back in the garden room, she gazed at the evidence of Daisy's presence: folders, papers, a notepad and pencil. Stray words caught her attention: Balmoral... Irene... She picked up the book with the hunting scene on the cover, the date on the spine...

She sat down, read, absorbed. When she had finished she sat still for some moments. Then she got up and went through the silent house. Her citadel, sometimes threatened, yet she had preserved its inviolability by simply doing nothing at all, a reflex inertia; protecting herself, her way of life, her family and those she loved.

She picked up the receiver. The ringing tone, the answerphone. 'Clive, answer, please, if you're there. I need to see you urgently —'

'Floy, I'm here. What is it?'

'You must come round at once, at once, Clive.'

It was a moment he had never believed would happen; he couldn't look at her, instead he stared down at papers, notebooks, scribbles. He turned pages, took in some sense from the written words, unnecessary words, his vision went beyond them, back to what had happened. He knew exactly what that was.

He said, 'Do you understand this, Floy?'

'You haven't been listening, Clive. Yes, I understand. Quill told me how Irene met her death, not at the time, but later. He told me that Hugh had proof. The photograph. At the time, I didn't want to know anything, and afterwards we never spoke of the matter, until recently, when it became unavoidable. And now

Daisy knows. Or is putting two and two together. Do you think she's done something impulsive?'

He said wearily, 'You just don't know impulsive when it comes to Daisy.' Because she didn't: she had never enquired into the truth behind the 'theft' of the Rover, remained in steady ignorance of Daisy's visit to the Skinners. Every protective act, every soothing dissimulation might never have occurred; all Floy knew was that she was safe behind Daisy's guard.

'But what do you think she might do?'

He said, 'Any bloody thing,' and immediately apologised.

They were talking evenly, without emotion, like polite strangers, she with the delicate confusion that was never far from her voice, whatever the circumstance. He was able to look at her then, see how her composed fragility was the essence of herself: she had never come to terms with the everyday, she had turned it into a sublime irrelevance, meaningful only when events swept her towards the necessary attitudes for survival.

This she now demonstrated, sitting beside him, picking up the journal, the unsuspected, treacherous, only too well understood narrative. 'She will, I think, have some idea of getting to the truth, however...' Distant murmuring about the undesirability of the matter being revived, things could go further, which would not do. The media interest in Quill's death...

'I rather think it's his life they're interested in,' Clive breathed.

Floy, valiantly protected from such publications, saying, 'We don't want his relationship, the nature of it, with Edward talked about. And that family – our – regrettable connection with them.'

'You mean,' he said carefully, 'we have to stop it all coming out now.'

'Yes.' In one gently uttered word all the monstrous blindness to reality – saving them from themselves. 'If we do something at once.'

'What?'

The priority was to find out where Daisy had gone, and here Floy displayed an unlikely efficiency, indicating phrases underlined, *Balmoral Drive*. 'She can't be there, the house is empty and Phyllis is now senile, Daisy knew that. Josie talked of it, she was here, quite recently, giving me news of her mother. Then she's underlined *across the road to Marjorie and Professor Cope*. There would be no point in her going there either – Marjorie moved years ago and Professor Cope died, oh, I can't recall when, but – *Well, I knew she'd be lecturing at the University but her cleaner was there*. And look, Daisy made this note, *Grandmother Skinner was the professor's cleaning lady*.

They were silent for a moment; Clive watched subtle changes of expression as she came to a decision. A slight tremor in her voice, 'These grandparents are harsh, bigoted, I don't want Daisy...bruising herself against them. They could be vindictive... You used to go to their house with Edward when you were boys...'

His knowledge of what happened on the Wednesday night of Quill's disappearance was limited, the only person who knew more was the murderer. Now he was forced to admit the unadmitted: Edward could somehow be implicated in Quill's death.

'Clive, you surely agree? We have to be practical.'

It would be the first time in her life. 'What?'

'You must see if Daisy's been there, to —' a vague gesture towards the unfamiliar word, the ungraspable concept, 'confront them.'

'We don't want to draw their fire.'

The irony lost on her. 'I'm sure you're right. You must go at once, find her, we don't know how long ago she left here.'

You used to go to their house with Edward...

The generality of Edward's family, ill-made people in cheap clothes, exercised a magnetic attraction with their raucous comradeship, garrulous feuds and habit of living in and out of each others' houses; the crudeness of the men, the accepted wildness of their criminality as something only to be expected. Whenever he had the chance (never daring to at home) he adopted their slovenly diction and swearing and yelpingly coarse laughter; in fevered fantasies he grappled with the precocious sexuality of the girls. He never gained acceptance amongst them but there was a rough acknowledgement of him as our Edward's mate – and accompanying deliberate smirks and nudges he hoped he didn't understand and made him blush scarlet.

But with the grandparents – that was being thrown to stalking animals. Visits were excruciating, Edward went only when commanded by his father and dragged Clive with him. Clive in enslavement, exposed himself to the misery of rudeness and suspicion he could respond to only with feeble humour, pretending it was all a joke. They never spoke directly to him, but only between themselves, loudly, referring to 'his lordship'. When they spoke to Edward it was in abrupt, barking comments, always about Irene. She was not a subject of enquiry or conversation, she was a reference of disparagement: 'Talking posh. Be that stepmother, she wears the trousers now.' 'Her ladyship'll be making you mind your manners.'

After Irene's death the visits became less frequent. They were not the kind of people to offer condolences, and the target of their oblique criticism having been removed, they never mentioned her; she became an embarrassed silence, with some lurking projection of resentment that she had deprived them of their fun.

Then when Edward's father became ill, the visits virtually stopped. Edward – always having prided himself on being able to handle his grandparents – 'I can take those two old buggers on' – became vulnerable, spent as much time as he could with Clive at Fairmead, talking a great deal to Floy about Irene, and how much he and his father missed her. Floy, knowing in detail every clash of temperament, was bemused but always kind.

After Stanley Crane's death the fiction took root, and immediately flourished, that the grandparents were sheltering and sustaining Edward in his orphaned state. 'He's always welcome under our roof.' Clive saw through that from the beginning. Far from making a home for him they left him to racket around with anyone who would have him, he was allowed under their roof only when family complications made it unavoidable. He was vengeful, narrow-eyed, threatening retribution; but on his behalf Clive felt an unspoken hurt that adults could treat a boy so.

Towards – or rather, deflected from – Clive, they adopted an insulting humour, incomprehensible remarks about her ladyship having to meet her dues and about time, and – with an effusiveness never before heard – to Edward, 'You're not losing out. You've got your own to see what's done fair. You're only a lad, there's obligations.'

Edward was going through a period of favour, as bizarre as it was inexplicable, treated by all his family with such exaggerated affection he seemed to spend entire days in bosomy embraces and showering sympathy. There had never been much notion of discipline, now he became lordly, pampered and sly, when Clive – conscious that 'her ladyship' only ever meant Aunt Irene – asked him what they were talking about he lisped with pantomime wide-eyed innocence, 'Don't know…'

As the weeks, then months went by, insensibly, the emotional atmosphere cooled, impatience and derision crept in. Clive, once the target of ridicule, might as well have become invisible; Edward now squirmed beneath the heavy scorn, barked or muttered, *Hell of a wait for this divvying up…somebody telling porkies about his fortune.* Whatever he attempted to say was either drowned by wordless jeers or smirkingly ignored. Did yer hear suffink? What? Nuffink as amounts to owt.

Clive, smarting on Edward's behalf, at last comprehended that Edward had assumed money would come to him from Irene. He was bewildered, as a boy he had no place in the monetary affairs or the family; Edward's demands that he do something, talk them round, met his helplessness and hurt on Edward's behalf. All he could do was stick by him, faithful when everyone else let him down. Flinging him off, Edward accused him of neglect, treachery, said one day they'd all pay – his own family, and the Mannerings.

He slowed before the house, his nerve failing, drove round the corner, facing away from the house, pulled up by the kerb between two lamp posts, one unlit.

He had been in a robotic state since the shock of discovering

Floy had always known about his part in Irene's death. Hiding from herself what she knew, never treating him with anything less than kindness and affection.

The bizarre replaying of the past, enmeshed now with Floy's uncharacteristic urgency, had severed so many rational processes he had simply done as she directed, without asking why. Now, sitting outside that house with all its humiliating memories, he wasn't even sure what he was doing there.

It was in darkness, upstairs and down, he could not have woken them, the Jaguar's engine purred too softly to disturb their sleep.

In spite of the years since he had been there, it was mapped on his memory: the starkly treeless streets, the monotonous sameness of the houses; behind them footpaths everywhere, bisecting the estate. When it had been built, no one had a car, people walked to work, to shop, to visit, walked between the gardens of their neighbours, between vegetables plots, bald lawns, roses pampered into winning modest prizes; painstakingly built small greenhouses. He had learnt to thread through them all in Edward's company, his daring and raw and voluptuous company, the people he knew engaged upon so many lawlessly exciting matters.

He was sitting, looking through his rear mirror at the darkened house, knowing that if he knocked they would not open the door. It was their way, the family always came in by the back door, if anyone knocked at the front, they peeked round the curtain edge, decided if they would or – on one painfully recalled occasion – would not answer. *It's her about her dead kid, it's no good going on talking, that'll not bring him back.* Voices just above a whisper. And another time: *If he's battered her again she'll have deserved it. We can't come between husband and wife.* And they all kept completely still until the human tragedy that had been desperate enough to seek pity, turned away from their door.

A flicker of movement in the mirror. Someone hurrying, soft-footed along the side road, disappearing into the footpath behind the houses. The swiftest glimpse, but unmistakable. Edward.

He sat stricken as lights came and went in sequence: the hall, the landing. Then in the cramped back bedroom where he and Edward – grandparents respectably absent – revelled in the sweat of sexual discovery.

By the time the light in the small, remembered room went out, he had made all the true and terrible connections.

He had to drive quite a way, make many attempts before he found a phone box that had not been vandalised.

Hunter held the telephone receiver away from the urgent voice. 'Clive, of course Daisy isn't with me, I'm in my office – what? Who? Look, just calm down. You're on the bypass by the Easton estate – and you've seen Edward – yes, just slow down – his grandparents – OK but what —' With the patience that characterised all his doings, Hunter attempted to sort out Clive's urgent recital, of course he would listen, Daisy's name was there —

An abrupt knock and Annette was in his office, so white-faced he was instantly concerned, he rose to his feet, barked, 'Clive, shut up, shut up a minute,' putting the receiver down on his desk. His tough, dependable officer had suffered some shock, there were guidelines about how to cope with this; for Hunter there was only the immediacy of comfort, male or female, what did it matter, 'Hey, come on, Annette…'

But she backed way, unaccountably distancing herself, saying helplessly, 'No, Mr Hunter – it's you – it's you…'

'What? What?'

'Sir. It's Daisy. I'm so sorry.'

And there was this abyss of unwanted understanding, in Annette's face, in her voice, in words he wished not to hear.

She's dead. She's dead.

No. No…

His arm was helplessly taken. As Annette led him out of his office they were all standing, silent, names known and half known, faces stricken as he walked down the corridor between them in silence, a man of stone.

The patrol car had been on the scene within minutes of Daisy's body being found. Once the news hit Talbot Way it was everywhere at reeling speed. PC Barlow, looking for ways to make himself useful, but so new he could only be on the edge of the long devoted loyalty, found himself in the stunned wake by Hunter's open office door. From a telephone receiver cast down on the desk, a voice shouted, 'Sheldon – listen – where are you for God's sake —'

Barlow picked the receiver up. 'Can I be of assistance, sir?'

'What? Who – Oh, I'm Clive Mannering —'

'Oh, yes, Mr Mannering. PC Barlow here, I came to see you...'

Provided with an opportunity for relentless efficiency, Barlow went at once to his Inspector with a rapid explanation and a direct lead to a stalled murder enquiry.

He stood on the railway bridge. Around him Annette and James, George Withers, Mary Clegg, so many others.

He looked down, saw her in the glare of the portable lighting, the grace of her death.

People spoke to him. Said...? Perhaps he answered.

But there were only two words: failure and heartbreak.

Chapter Twenty-Nine

Hunter's boss, Superintendent Garret, sympathetic, but always pragmatic. 'Sheldon, you know you can't handle any aspect of this investigation.'

Of course he knew. Edward's arrest had taken place when he was in the blighted state of comprehending Daisy's death. When he began to make sense of anything – beyond the determination to one day get his hands round Edward's throat – he accepted he could have no input into the conduct of the investigation: interviewing, charging, court procedure…

'Think, when it gets to court, what would happen to you there? What sort of credibility would you personally have? You were going to marry her, for God's sake, everyone knew it. Sheldon, you stay away from Edward Crane, if you go anywhere near him you'll prejudice the entire show. And stay away from that bloody Skinner family, and everyone we believe was assisting him, the slightest suggestion you've interfered with witnesses —'

It was what he would have said, in the Super's position…

But I am in a world without her.

'We weren't even looking for Edward Crane. If it hadn't been for Mannering he could have slipped through our fingers, but because he shopped him and Barlow acted we got to him straight away. That's one cocksure bastard, Sheldon – claimed he'd only been round the corner posting a letter and apart from those few minutes his grandparents could swear he'd been there all evening. And you know they deny Daisy was ever there at all.'

'Are they still sticking to that?'

'So far. He never had time to dispose of his clothes – never occurred to him we'd catch him so quickly – at all, even. He's convinced he can get away with anything. None of them seem to appreciate the weight of the forensic case against —'

It'll take time to put together…

…particles of her body and clothes on…

…arrested and charged with two murders…

Fragments of cognition. She had received a crushing blow to

her head before being pushed on to the railway line, she had fought…

He knew her supple strength, but then, her fragility.

…They had been on the old bridge that was undergoing repair, littered with jagged lumps of masonry…

Daisy, my beloved girl.

The case against Edward was building up inexorably. A man he had never set eyes on in the flesh, who belonged in the memory and knowledge and experience of others.

'Claude Jennings has taken over from you —' Hunter knew him, from Headquarters, a caustic and scrupulous man. 'The priority is we nail Crane. So, Sheldon, I feel for you, you know that, and you know I have your welfare at heart, but – stay clear. All right?'

He saw him out, hand on his shoulder. 'This is doubly hard for you because you're just about the most hands-on copper I've ever come across. And you're one of our own. There are,' he paused, 'other routes.'

He knew that, too. He would take no compassionate leave, he would go insane unoccupied. His day to day job meant he was constantly present at Talbot Way, and everyone talked to him: CID, uniform, the murder enquiry team. And in the pub; phoning his flat in the evening, and if he couldn't be persuaded to come out, chatting endlessly, always about the progress of the investigation. He observed with black humour that he had never had so much input, from so many sources.

A tired and empty evening. He opened the door of his flat and Clive was there. Mirrored on both their faces the stolid worn despair. Hunter told him, with justifiable profanity, that whatever he had to say had to be done officially, that he had been rendered helpless and grieving by the self preserving, purblind tradition of the Mannerings. 'You know you can't talk to me officially and I certainly don't want to see you personally.'

'I understand that.'

'Good. Fuck off.'

'Yes, Sheldon, yes. I've done everything I can officially, I've spent hours with your lot, I've told them everything I know and can think of, but I need to tell you, for Daisy's sake, and yours,'

Hunter's apartment had always been an impersonal place, except, too briefly, for her glimmering self. Clive, by unwitting association, brought a whisper of her grace, her elegance. Hunter hated him for it. Hated him for all those years squandered by people who had known her and not known how to value and protect her. He had become repetitive, 'Explain. Or fuck off.'

Clive explained. Hunter, in monolithic silence, listened.

'On the evening Quill was expected at Fairmead, I was at home, alone. I had a phone call. From Edward. He said he was calling from Chatfield Central, about to get on the train to London, and it was vital I meet Quill, he had something very important to tell me and to give me, he couldn't say what, someone was listening. He said I had to drive straight away to Merlin Mere, Quill was already on his way there and I was to wait for him in the lay-by off the Rush Deeping road. Then he put the phone down.

'That's where I was, the night Quill disappeared. When your people came to see me, I was in an absolute funk. And then, when Quill's – body – was found, I knew I was into something I couldn't handle. It was worse still when you turned up that photograph. I unearthed a couple of long-ago numbers, trying to contact Edward but I couldn't trace him – he just seemed to have disappeared. He'd always been good at that.

'When Floy summoned me round to Fairmead and showed me Mrs Twemlowe's diary, I was desperate. I didn't think Daisy could be in any danger, on my word of honour, Sheldon. I didn't. I drove round a while, looking for her, then I went to Edward's grandparents. Floy wanted me to find out if Daisy had been there – but I knew them. I knew no matter how long I knocked they'd never answer. Then, as I was sitting in my car, I saw Edward.

'He hadn't gone *anywhere*, he was there *all the time*. That wild goose chase he'd sent me on was to make sure I had no alibi. I never thought what anything had to do with Daisy finding out about Irene's death. When I saw him slip into his grandparents' house by the back way everything – telescoped – the understanding…

'That's when I phoned you. I realised Edward had to have something to do with Quill's death – and you were the only one who could get the truth out of him. You put the phone down, I was shouting, after a while someone spoke to me, a PC Barlow —'

Hunter stopped listening to the painstaking explanation. He knew just how PC Barlow's immediate action had resulted in Edward's arrest, knew the Manor's receptionist picked Edward out at the identity parade – that put him in the frame right from the start.

It was true he had been kept up to date with everything, the smallest, inconsequential detail, but it had all come to him from arm's length, this was his first chance of direct questioning. Clive, a lifelong friend of the woman Hunter intended to marry, could be termed a personal friend, he was unlikely to tell anyone what passed between them.

There was a certain cold comfort in professionalism; he had absorbed and evaluated everything Clive had said; his questioning began, methodical, exact.

'What was Edward doing in Chatfield the night he phoned you?'

'He didn't say. His relationship with Quill was volatile. I assumed they'd got together again and it was the usual arrangement – he'd travelled with Quill and then visited his family.'

'Then he told you Quill had something important to tell you and – to give you. What did you understand by that?'

'I thought – it had to be the photo, surfacing after all this time —'

'Why?'

'Weeks ago, Quill phoned when I was with Daisy at Floy's. Brenda was there, inflicting herself on Floy. She and Edward have an unholy alliance, she passes on anything she can to him, enlists her family – after that they made a nuisance of themselves, asking about Quill visiting Hugh. Something was in the wind, I just ignored it.'

Of course you did. Perfect gentleman, adored by Daisy. I think I'll murder you as a surrogate for Edward.

'He said he couldn't talk because someone was listening. Who do you think he meant?'

'One of his damn family, secrecy's second nature to him.'

'Right. He told you to drive straight away to Merlin's Mere. Oh, come on, Merlin's Mere. Condom corner. Who's going to see you there?'

'Yes, but that was the point. I drove for half an hour down winding lanes and sat in a deserted lay-by for – Sheldon, for God's sake, who *would* see me?'

No one, easily. A place where every nook, every clump of bushes or trees had a car tucked beneath, beside; it could be crammed with seethingly copulating pairs but no one would look at anyone else – unless they'd gone there specifically for that purpose. Further confirmation that only someone who knew the area would send Clive there. Fair enough.

'The next day you hear Quill is missing, then his body was found. Why didn't you ask the Skinners if they'd seen Edward?'

He sighed, 'They'd tell me lies or nothing, he was playing his own game. After I spoke to Mrs Caffrey, I tried to work out what it was.'

'She's Quill's housekeeper.'

'Yes. He'd phoned her the day Quill travelled —'

'Daisy told me, he was abusive. How did he know Quill was on his way here? He'd left him, hadn't he?'

'It seems only a fortnight before. I went over to Wicklow last week to see Quill's solicitor, help with all the necessary arrangements. I had a talk with Mrs Caffrey. She'd overheard an arrangement that when Quill visited Hugh, Edward would go with him. Then Edward just – took off. Even so, he phoned every day, whatever the calls were about Quill was always upset afterwards and he became very nervous. I think Edward was checking up on him, and quite possibly threatening him.'

Hunter didn't ask, 'About what?' His look yielded nothing.

'Edward had to get his hands on the photograph, it was the one bargaining tool left. His relationship with Quill was washed up, Hugh was beyond reach as far as blackmail was concerned – but there was one sitting duck left, one source of extortion – Floy.

And all the time that photograph had never surfaced. That meant Hugh still had it. And he wanted to see Quill for the last time, give it to him, tell him the truth.

'Edward knew Quill's travel plans, so he came here first, somewhere, I don't know, to be on the spot. But Quill gave him the slip. Edward would never have thought he'd dare, and he must have been snarling. By the time he caught up with him at the Manor, Quill was already with Hugh.'

Yes. They thought about this, parallel scenarios. After a silence, Hunter said, 'So he set you up.'

Clive nodded, quelled by betrayal. 'He could always think fast.'

'Went outside and waited.'

'Yes.'

Hunter put everything on his mental file. Evaluated it.

'This isn't just about that sodding photograph, is it?' And when Clive shook his head, 'What, then?'

'It started when we were boys, with Irene's accident. Edward told me we could be accused of murder. I was terrified. He said we had to stick together and he'd look after me. For years I told myself it was a sacred friendship, we championed each other, there was even a kind of honour in our silence – keeping the good name of people who cared for us. The truth was I was besotted with him, overwhelmed, his daring, his sexuality.'

Hunter watched him speaking from a revisited time, frightened and detailed, now rushing back to beset him, this boyish past.

'He hated Irene for taking his mother's place. It was no good saying that his father needed a kind and loving wife. He'd longed for that camera, Stanley couldn't afford to buy him one. Irene did, and he hated her for that too. Such a savage irony to record her death with it.'

'That photograph was a time bomb. Why in God's name didn't Hugh destroy it?'

He shrugged, 'I don't know. It was me it threatened. On its evidence, Quill always believed I was the one responsible for Irene's death.'

'It was as much evidence against Edward as you – he had to be there to take it.'

'That was it – I think they contained him by it. Years later he came to me for money, threatened to make it public. I told him to go ahead, I could tell he was bluffing. Neither of them would have been mad enough to hand it over to him.'

'But he was able to use it against them.'

'Oh, yes. I was never sure how upset he really was over his father's death. He was furious when he found out Irene had left them no money, he'd somehow led his family to think they'd all be well off, and when eventually no one got anything, they behaved disgracefully, they never gave him any comfort, made fun of him, *blamed* him —' A sudden bitterness: his own and Edward's humiliation meeting on common ground.

'He said he'd get even with them all... There were lots of

things I never understood then, and later didn't want to. But if perhaps, now Daisy…'

It burst from Hunter, from his contained grief. 'Daisy tried, didn't she? Completely in the dark, while you had so many pieces you could have fitted together. She didn't have these *secrets*, the passionate suburban despair, what is not said, because it's not respectable, manageable. She knew the rules, the behaviour and manners and attitudes, but she tried to protect Floy —'

Then he had to turn away, he had never found any satisfaction in seeing a man cry.

He went to the sideboard, poured two glasses of Glenmorangie, when he turned back Clive, some composure regained, tucked away his handkerchief. 'I do apologise.'

'OK.' *Do you know how much weeping I've done?*

They sat there in the shreds of their dignity and helpless anger, each bearing his own desolation – yes, he probably did, he was doubly bereaved, a relative and a dear friend. Hunter said, 'Go on.'

'I stuck by him, but he began pushing me into things I didn't want to do, letting me down, cadging. Then he told me Hugh and Quill between them had settled something for him. He wouldn't say what, he was triumphant, mysterious, powerful…'

'Blackmail?'

'That's all I can think of. So much they didn't want to come to light – Hugh's relationship with him, Irene's death, Quill trying to protect me and Floy – endless opportunities for Edward to manipulate us all. I suppose they just paid him off. Perhaps when he was eighteen, that's when he left home – the last thing he'd do was let any of his family get a sniff of his money. He's still always had a hold over Quill, he's battened on him these last few years – I'd say he expects to be Quill's heir, I don't know, I haven't had a look at the will yet. But if Quill found out the truth from Hugh…'

'Did he, though? According to Daisy, Hugh wasn't making any sense.'

'Yes, well, perhaps it was his last lucid moment, we'll never know. What is certain, Quill didn't get the photo. And Edward – you can't imagine his rages —'

An intimation of something not quite right, put aside for another time:

'He knew Chatfield better than I ever have. He knew where to go without being seen, who to bully or bribe or cajole into helping him, how to cover his tracks…'

Hunter recognised the signs. Clive, shriven, had run out of words and emotional stamina, he could no longer explain anything because his narrative had returned him to his first, giddying love; Edward, inhabitant of the penumbra around lives, actions, intentions. Edward, threat and charm, persuasion and ruthlessness. A cheat, a fraud, a liar. Now a killer.

Hunter poured more whisky. Clive stared down, swirling his glass. 'This is the absolute truth, Sheldon, and I don't care if you believe it or not. I told you we found Irene lying on the pavement. We didn't.' He paused, gathering himself for the final confession.

Hunter, with bleak satisfaction, spared him the effort. 'Did you really think I'd fall for that?'

'No, well, you're professionally tuned to sniff out liars.'

'You did it, didn't you? Played the game.'

'Yes. The first, the only time. And do you know what? My nerve failed. I couldn't do it to Irene – I couldn't do it to anyone. Edward shot ahead – I saw him level with her – he – nudged. It only took that – his speed, strength, her unsteadiness. He told me he'd wobbled, and I pretended to believe him.'

In the exhausted pause, Hunter heard the authentic voice of long delayed confession. Yes, Clive was telling the truth.

'It was nerve-wracking afterwards, the enquiries, if there were any witnesses. But there weren't. We'd got away with it.'

Hunter nodded. He hadn't been sure till then that his seemingly inconsequential knowledge of a past event gave him an advantage, allowed him to savour the bitter aloes of satisfaction, transferring his suffering where it belonged. 'Not quite. There was one.'

'What? A witness?' Clive's polite contradiction. 'No, you're mistaken, Sheldon. No one ever came forward.'

'She wouldn't.'

'Who?'

'Edward's grandmother.'

After a long, speechless stare, Clive muttered, 'What do you mean?'

When Hunter had told him he spoke, his voice thick, talking to himself, 'She knew. She'd have told – they knew it was Edward – and they kept quiet – all these years, they let – believe —'

'Wait a minute, wait a minute. If you're trying to tell me you never knew... But you read Mrs Twemlowe's diary —'

'Read it? I wasn't in a state to read anything, I don't think I took in a word.'

'What did you think it was about?' Hunter asked carefully.

'About? About Floy finding out after all these years what we'd done, Edward and me. I'd never been able to bear the thought of her ever knowing, I'd hidden it from myself, buried it. And suddenly – she confronted me. I never even suspected that damn diary existed, and later that same evening, your people took it away. I haven't seen it since, or spoken to Floy about it.'

After a puzzled pause, 'So why did you go to the grandparents?'

'Because Floy said Daisy had gone there, if she told me why – no, I don't think she did – I never took it in. She might have assumed I'd worked it all out, the way she had. But she'd had time, to realise... She just said I had to see if Daisy had gone to the grandparents, make sure she was all right.' He repeated, 'All right,' coming upon a diverted thought. 'His grandparents, they've given him his alibi, haven't they? Yes, they would, perjure themselves, they're afraid of him, he treats them like shit, why not, that's the way they treated him, when he was a boy, and defenceless. No, it's no excuse —'

Through every pressure, every calamity, Clive had kept the countenance of a gentleman, now, in a naked moment, a savagely angry man stared at Hunter. '*And they let Edward loose on Daisy.*'

The next day Hunter sought out DCI Jennings, Annette was with him. 'Have you talked to Floy about Daisy?'

'Not yet, apparently she's not been well enough to see us. Annette, you up to date?'

'Yes. She's been staying with her neighbour —'

Hunter nodded, 'Grace Wilmot. Nice sensible woman.'

Annette said, 'She says Floy's much better now. I've fixed up we'll see her this morning.' It was sometimes painfully difficult talking to him, she couldn't ask if he'd seen Floy, she hadn't heard him mention her name till now. It was unlikely Floy knew anything, but as one of the last people to see Daisy alive she had to be interviewed.

'OK. Clive Mannering came to see me yesterday evening.'

Jennings asked, 'What for?'

'I think he wants me to forgive him,' Hunter said tonelessly. Neither of them asked if he had. 'And amongst other things…' He repeated carefully everything Clive had said, much of it already known. But not the blackmail. The possibility had been built into the situation from the beginning, Clive had no proof – just the soured recognition that Edward would never pass up an opportunity. But he seemed not to have taken it for several years after Irene's death. Why wait for his 'settlement?'

They worked through it. He was just as guilty as Clive, there was no way he could deny that. Two frightened boys, helpless to do anything except keep quiet, and wait for everything to go back to normal. Then Edward's father died, he had to adjust to that, to being an orphan with nothing now except the indifference and scorn of his family. But time went by, and the acceptance that the 'accident' was just that and no more, brought with it the delayed discovery he did have power, after all.

He had always, according to Clive, 'on a piffling scale', extorted money and presents from Hugh; chance had put him into a mannered, polite world where a civic minded gentleman fostered talent in the young, true, but Clive knew the reality behind the façade. He really didn't care what Hugh was up to with Edward, and he wasn't programmed to blackmail. When Edward was old enough and ready to make his demands, he extorted enough from Hugh to strike out on his own. Years later, he and Quill met again, he moved in with Quill.

Which brought them to the point, why did Edward murder Quill? Hunter said, 'According to Clive, Edward regarded himself as Quill's heir, if Quill had found out *he* was the one responsible for Irene's death – Quill would have cut him out completely.'

Annette, always trying to follow Hunter's mind, asked him if he believed that.

'It's feasible. But no, I think there's something else. For a start, how many blackmailers murder their victims?'

'To stop Quill altering his will,' Annette suggested.

'That's what Clive thinks. But, the original blackmail, it wasn't only Hugh in danger of losing out. Quill was his best friend, two men and two boys. Clive claims his relationship with Quill was totally innocent, and he's sure the same went for Edward. I believe him. That wouldn't stop Edward threatening to accuse them both though, would it? He could have landed them both in prison. Edward's vicious when he can away with it. But he's self preserving, a survivor. Maybe, as Clive thinks, it was just rage —'

Annette saw how tired he was, how his haunted sleepless nights had left him hollowed inside the shell of his duty, his abstract sense of justice. It seemed to her that all that was carrying him from one day to the next was his personal determination to see Daisy's murderer called to account.

'Claude, that diary of Mrs Twemlowe —'

Jennings said, 'Sheldon, we've been over this, it has no relevance to the present investigation, there's nothing we can use —'

Hunter agreed. It wasn't relevant to the current charges, it could do nothing except clog up the flow, the woman who wrote it, the only witness to an unrecorded crime, was now incapable. Added to that was his wry inward acknowledgement that that was why they'd handed it over to him, to keep him occupied, stop him going ape.

'I'm not suggesting, Claude, it has weight to merit time being spent on it, and even if anyone had trawled through it, only someone with an intimate knowledge, familiarity with family connections would have come on the relevance. Daisy did.'

Jennings leaned back with a politely disguised sigh. Annette looked down at her hands.

'Clive never knew the grandmother was a witness, he nearly had a seizure when I told him. When he'd calmed down, we talked about it, and he has no idea if Edward knew she'd seen them, he'd certainly never hinted anything like it.'

'If I listen carefully,' Jennings said, 'can I hear the sound of scores being settled?'

'Clive would use anything in accord with his gentlemanly integrity to get Edward banged up forever. So would I. Delete the gentlemanly. The thing is, did Edward think his grandmother believed in his innocence all these years? Or have they been in collusion? Either way, it's something to lean on them both with.'

'Sheldon, I've always thought you were as subtle as a brick through a window. Now I realise I'm the brick. How I'm going to sort my way through this and get a result, I don't know.'

'Try putting Annette on it. Or James. Or even Mary Clegg. As someone once said, they're unbeatable truffle hounds.'

In the garden room at Fairmead, DCI Jennings and Annette sat with Floy. Hesitant, her gaze hunting for all the lost certainties, she answered their questions about the last evening she had seen Daisy, verifying and corroborating Clive's account and then, from her brittle dignity, said something unsuspected, unknown. Anonymous letters.

Their advantage was the detail Hunter had gleaned from Clive, they could use what was relevant, discard what was not; if there had been a hint of anonymous letters, he would not have missed it. This brought an unspoken doubt: had double bereavement, scandal, disgrace, tipped this dignified lady over the edge? Jennings had already learnt to leave things to Annette when there was some pussy-footing to be done.

Annette leaned forward, querying, 'Miss Mannering, no one has so far…er, anonymous…?'

If there was such a thing as ethereal precision, Floy Mannering embodied it. She had the date when the first letter arrived. Two days after the visit of Mrs Brenda Hutton, Edward's aunt. It was written in an uneducated hand, mis-spelt, and told her that if she allowed Quill to visit Hugh, a member of her family would be charged with the murder of her sister Irene.

DCI Jennings, a direct man, patience tried by so much in this investigation of the boomeranging past, said, 'This letter, Miss Mannering. Will you show it to us?'

'I'm sorry, no. I destroyed it. There was another, later, in the same vein. That, too, I destroyed.'

Annette said, 'This accusation of murder, that's – it must have been devastating. What did you make of it?'

Floy was silent, distant, looking down at her fingers pleating her lace handkerchief. A woman composed of manners and sweetness, obligations and evasions – gave the merest sigh, and explained.

She had always known there was something not right about the boys' alibi. On that afternoon she had been having tea in the garden of a friend's house near the Quadrant and seen them, cycling in all the vitality of youth, only minutes before Irene's death. And when, afterwards, they claimed to be at Alderley Edge – she preferred not to make any sense of that. Clive was so deeply distressed by Irene's death, and she had the evidence of her own eyes that he had been in the vicinity at the time. She tried, in her own way, to encourage him to confide in her, but he never did.

And he had been with Edward. Edward was inseparable from trouble, lies, unsavoury episodes. She suspected Clive was shielding him, he did it often, bartering his decent behaviour and values for the approval of his friend.

It was true Edward deserved consideration, in view of his unfortunate domestic circumstances...

In present terms the word would be dysfunctional, Annette thought, but Floy had not yet discovered the present and never would. She was telling them, in essence, what Hunter had told them, but in a curiously desiccated fashion, her words parched of feeling.

Edward's relatives had baseless expectations of money coming to him from Irene. Perhaps the idea had come from Edward himself, it was just the sort of unrealistic notion that would plant itself in a schoolboy mind, and when it came to nothing his family all but disowned him. Aware of her obligations to Irene, she paid his school fees and saw that he was decently clothed. Beyond that he was his family's responsibility, not hers.

In time, he became ungovernable, insolent and vulgar, taking it as his right to be constantly at Fairmead, to bring his family with him. His mere presence nerve-racking, he was barred and Clive's parents also put their house out of bounds. He began to lose his influence over Clive, and eventually, he went away. If they continued to keep in touch she had no knowledge or interest. It was some years later he entered into a relationship with Quill, which she could not ignore, but would not engage with in any way. There were, inevitably, over time, superficial contacts, a telephone call, a chance encounter, no more.

She stopped speaking, removed her attention – uncannily, absolutely; it was as if she had left the room. Such a wisp of a woman, immaculately insubstantial, would they have noticed if she had? Annette asked, 'Shall I get you a glass of water?'

The shadow of a smile, shake of the head.

They seemed to have strayed from the anonymous letters, but no, Annette recognised the template, defined by Hunter: the pattern of the past shaping present events.

Jennings asked, 'Miss Mannering, what did you do about these anonymous threats?'

Do? The imperative was the good name of the family which would not allow her to speak to anyone, not even Daisy, whom she trusted absolutely, but who was protective and impetuous. She could not tell Clive that she was being coerced into a truth she had never wished to know.

She did nothing.

Dragging some practicality into the procedure, Jennings asked, 'Was there a postmark?'

'Cheshire. But it had to be Edward.'

'Why?'

'Only two people could possibly have known anything about my sister's death. Clive, an anonymous – no, unthinkable. And Edward. The threat came from him. His family were instrumental in some way, I don't know how, but he had always used them.'

When Jennings, searching for sanity, asked how they could have gone about it, she gave the slightest lift of her slim shoulders, said she had no way of understanding the practicalities. Into the silence that followed, Annette attempted a few.

'Edward Crane could have sent the sealed letter in another envelope, to one of his family, with instructions, probably over the phone, for them to address it to you, stamp and post it. This way, they wouldn't know what the letter said, and couldn't use its contents to apply any direct pressure on you. It was —' Annette added forthrightly 'unlike him to give up an advantage, he'd hardly hand over to them a means of blackmailing you.'

Floy regarded her with dazed admiration. 'I could never have constructed that myself, but yes, it is logical.'

Jennings said, 'It would have to be someone he could trust,

who'd keep quiet and not let him down. Who do you think that might be?'

Her distaste at speaking of any single member of the family registered in her silence.

'Please think,' Annette said. 'It would help us a great deal.'

This was a faint surprise to her, 'Help? I feel like a leaf blown by the wind.' But she thought, then offered, 'His aunt Brenda, she's a domineering woman. Or his grandparents, they are implacable.'

Jennings' question, 'Why should this happen now?' met with a response so blank she might as well have said, *You want me to explain all this?*

Annette took it on herself to interpret for Jennings, 'Thing is, Miss Mannering, Edward could have accused Clive at any time since your sister's death. But he didn't. Can you think, why now?' After another bewildered look she used the information Hunter had passed on from Clive. 'You mentioned Brenda. We understand that she waş here when Sir Aquilla rang you from Ireland and said he was thinking of coming to visit Hugh Stephenson. And it was two days after that the first letter came?'

At no time had Floy questioned how they knew so much about her personal life; she must have simply assumed their knowledge was limitless. After a pause, turning everything over in her mind or simply looking through the window at the consolation of her garden, she nodded, began to speak again in the same dispassionate way.

Quill had phoned her again a few days later, explaining that although he and Edward had ended their association, and he had no idea where Edward was, Edward had begun to telephone every day, adamant he must accompany Quill to the Manor. This was so obviously undesirable, he decided to cancel his visit. She would not trespass on his domestic arrangements, but she had to tell him how, dismayingly, some of the Skinners had been round asking about when he intended to see Hugh. With a sense that he was beleaguered quite as much as her, she agreed at once when he asked her to let it be known he had cancelled his visit.

After subsequent telephone conversations, she gathered

matters had not improved for him. For herself, harassed to the point of desperation, she told him then about the anonymous letters. He was shocked, full of sympathy, it was now imperative he see Hugh. He knew from previous visits to the Manor that once shown into Hugh's room, privacy would be assured. He therefore decided to travel two days before his announced travel date. He could rely entirely on her to keep this arrangement between themselves.

Of course he could. Her dearest, closest cousin, a man of honour, was threatened by the very qualities that made him generous, affectionate, loyal. He had for so long been hopelessly under Edward's spell, it was an understandable human weakness, if one had not met Edward one couldn't understand his attraction.

Alarm vibrated between Annette and Jennings – how securely is she attached to reality? Annette had been interviewing Edward daily. Hadn't this seeped into her? DCI Jennings palpably at a loss. Neither of them, with unspoken assent, found Edward *faintly* attractive.

And how will Edward lose out on the truth being revealed? It was not as bludgeoning a question as: why did Edward murder Quill, and Floy didn't hesitate, fumble for her place in the sequence; her vision had never shifted from the past.

Some time after Irene's death, when Edward had endured the danger of discovery, the trauma of his father's death, the rejection of his family – he found his own resources. They were simple and crude.

He could go to the police and say both Hugh and Quill had behaved inappropriately with him. It was not true as far as it concerned Quill, but that didn't matter, he had the power to make it true.

Jennings, dazed into momentary diversion, had accepted that Miss Mannering was, at last, well enough to be interviewed. But where on the range of human responses did this gossamer existence interact with the everyday, the unvarnished chapter and verse of need, greed, compromise?

If Edward persisted in his accusation, both Hugh and Quill

would have gone to prison. Prison. Their families, their reputations, their livelihoods, their lifetimes of earned achievement – destroyed. Forever.

Edward was so young, his impetus was the enjoyment of money to spend, at once, unsupervised. But he had all the more defined instincts of adversity, he knew his strength. Insurance. For the future.

Floy was unmarried and childless. Edward was Irene's stepson. Then the Mannering wealth, everything, should go to him on Floy's death.

This was what Quill put to her. As long as no one knew he was in a humiliating and dangerous situation, and she agreed, everything was folded away from the common gaze: the truth of Irene's death, Hugh's relationship with Edward, Edward's ability to destroy Quill.

That was what Edward had to lose. If Quill found out Clive was innocent, Edward wouldn't stand a chance of getting a penny from Floy.

Jennings drew breath, said, 'In view of all recent events, you have changed your will, Miss Mannering, just to —'

'Changed it? No.'

A breathing pause; they exchanged a glance. She didn't notice, she was looking into her own abstractions.

'There was no need, I never left anything to Edward. I told Quill I had, and the condition on which I agreed to do so was that he assured Edward he had seen my will. He hadn't. You see, Quill was far too honourable to doubt my word.'

It was the most sedate treachery, suspended in silence until she murmured, 'Quite simply, I lied.'

George Withers, worried ragged by Hunter's withdrawn state, said unarguably, 'Sheldon, we've known each other since before we could walk. We need a bit of time, you and me, you're getting a sight too far out of reach.'

'George, you've got things to do —'

'Not this evening.' He had cancelled his bowls practice.

They went to the stately, aldermanship quiet of the Union Hotel, had just settled with a bottle of claret when Hunter noticed another place set.

'That lass,' George said, 'Annette. She'll bring you up to date. You'll never bloody settle without.' It was what Hunter called George's flying by the seat of his pants psychology.

Annette's arrival coincided with the menu. They ordered steak and ale pie with roast potatoes and local vegetables. Yes, she had an update – to no detriment to her appetite, George heartily observed. She had to keep her strength up.

Amongst the latest developments, Nosy Skinner's lock-up, pin-pointed by Mary Clegg, had been searched, deposits on the tyres of Quill's car matched those on the floor of the garage, this was unarguably where his BMW had been the night of his murder. Edward, refusing to admit he even knew of the existence of the place, said of course his fingerprints were all over Quill's car, he'd been driving it for almost a year, hadn't he?

As for the lock-up, Nosy Skinner was prepared to swear it was in the keeping of the entire population of Chatfield, if he'd ever set foot in it himself, he couldn't recall. Edward, with his Cheshire cat smile, asked them what else did they expect, he was bound to have the support of all his family.

But he was wrong about that, the Skinners had begun to fall out amongst themselves – sparks of suspicion about each other, more vitally about Edward. There were too many lower ranks to whom Edward was a distant figure with a privileged lifestyle they had no share in.

His grandparents were the exception, immovable in their insistence that he was with them the night of Quill's murder. He had arrived, feeling off colour, on the noon of that day, spent his time watching television and reading newspapers. He didn't want to be bothered with the rest of the family, so they told no one he was there, he left the following afternoon. He was again with them from 'teatime' on the evening of Daisy's death. He knew nothing about Daisy calling; if she had done so it was during the few moments he went out to post a letter. His grandparents were in bed when he got back.

Apart from these specific times, he was vague, changing his movements, forgetting, suddenly recalling visits to meaningless locations, which he insisted on detailing minutely. But he was too concerned with his own cleverness to realise these twists and turns made nonsense of his grandparents' evidence. Every variation was passed on to them for their verification; they were old, bemused, and not telling the truth – soon enough that had to be their only recourse. Their grandson was on a double count of murder, they had already been warned that they were liable to be charged with conspiring to pervert the course of justice, and to think very carefully of the consequences. This abstract march of the judicial process had so little to do with their everyday life they seemed incapable of grasping its significance, even its reality. Confronted with the written proof that she had witnessed Irene's death and Edward's role in it, Grandmother's response was the immediately self-damning assertion that Edward would never let on about that, and anyway, there's the photograph of that nancy Clive.

Annette, with either Jennings or Collier, had regularly interviewed them. She recounted each session to Hunter, telling him only so much as she knew would come to him from other sources; a great deal she and James agreed to keep from him. They soon became helplessly aware that other people were not so tactful. Initially the grandparents denied Daisy had called on them on the night of her death; Grandmother challenged, 'Where are your witnesses, then? Found someone as saw her, have you? Where are they, then?'

Edward?

Oh no, did they think she was a half-wit, trying to catch her out like that? He'd never say nothing, and anyway he'd gone out to post a letter…

Grandfather, interviewed separately, grew rancorous, said no one had a right to come knocking at their door, committing common trespass, accusing honest folk. What did it matter what had happened when Edward was no more than a child? Louder, boastfully insulting: and what business was it of hers, that Daisy slut, anyway. They'd shown her she couldn't get away with treating them like dirt, they'd brought her off her high horse, right down, sent her about her business…

James and Annette listened grimly, punctuating the increasing incoherence with an occasional question. It must have been quite a row, how long was she there? In his grey face Grandfather's faded eyes grew sharp. They'd not let that little cow over doorstep. Oh no. Went off, she did, straight away, our Edward saw her driving off in her car, coming back from post. He'd not want to be reminded by the likes of her about years ago, when he'd been ruined by that old sir something.

Didn't he mean Hugh Stephenson?

Him as well. Taking advantage of a helpless lad. And those Mannerings, cheating him, well, they'd got their come-uppance, name all over the papers, everyone knowing about him in Ireland…

Annette, savouring the last mouthful of superb meat gravy, said, 'Guv, you don't need me to tell you how mind-numbing it is listening to an almost demented old bugger shouting the odds.'

'Yes,' Hunter said. 'Go on.'

With a surreptitiousness remarkable for so large a man, George put his hand on hers under the table. He knew. Suddenly they were both sure Hunter did, by now.

'The old boy said Daisy had driven herself to the railway station, and the disgrace, and —' Annette faltered, 'she'd killed herself.'

Topped herself. Serve her right, trying to blame others. It was that nancy boy Clive did it anyway…

A thought too painful to bear, Daisy's joyous engagement in life, the woman he had loved with his whole heart. Worse, her last moments at the mercy of those two old monsters.

Yes, he knew. He would bear the pain, her pain.

She went on, faltered, 'The grandfather – he said Edward had told them that was what she'd done. We asked him when – he said "afterwards", then he couldn't remember. It was a hell of job trying to disentangle his time scale. We checked with the old girl's statement; Edward had got them word perfect, but they're out of their depth.'

George said, 'What it is, at last we've established Edward wasn't present when Daisy spoke to them. 'Afterwards' could only mean when he got back from the railway station. Annette's right, before we got round to the house he had time to coach them, just to be on the safe side. He'd never have admitted what he'd done, he'd have spun them some line. He was giving them chapter and verse, to be on the safe side. It'll make no odds, he'll never get away with that as a defence, and we've got the weight of forensic evidence.'

'He's trying to say it's all rigged.'

'Aye, and he'll not get away with that, either. And they have changed their version of the night Quill was murdered. Now they're saying they believed he was in his room, if he went out, they didn't hear.'

Hunter nodded. He had a vast silence inside himself, sometimes it settled on him tangibly, and everyone went quiet around him. Annette wondered how he managed it when he was alone, perhaps he was afraid of it. Before her helplessness and George's became evident, the waiter brought the pudding list. The supreme comfort food, jam roly poly, treacle tart, apple suet dumplings.

George said, 'Sheldon tells me you and Mr Jennings went to Fairmead today. Anything interesting?'

'You could say that,' Annette murmured – Hunter had been waiting for her when she got back.

When she got to the anonymous letters George said, 'By heck, are you sure? I mean, you said she's a bit, well, vague?'

'She'd have no reason to make them up.' Annette didn't voice the gloomy thought that Daisy had been right all the time – something had been very wrong. How often did Hunter say that to himself?

The will had the same surprise element. George regarded Hunter, calculating, 'You thought there were something else. Was that it? Crane believed he was going to inherit from her. *Everything —*'

'Because that's what Quill believed,' Annette said. 'Then, well, I think he found out Clive was innocent.'

'That's why Crane murdered him,' George said.

After a pause, Hunter said quietly, 'But Quill was wrong, wasn't he? Edward had never been in line to inherit anything from Floy.'

They turned over the implications of this. George was the first to speak. 'Hell of a thought, isn't it? Quill accepted her word...'

Nobody said, *if he hadn't, he'd still be alive.* But Hunter asked Annette, 'Did you, or Claude, point that out to Floy?'

'No, Mr Jennings didn't consider it relevant to the matter in hand. It must have been staring her in the face, but she'd look away. She knows how to do that, just like the Skinners.'

'And when it comes to dirty fighting,' George murmured, 'there doesn't seem much to choose between them.'

They ate pudding in philosophical silence. Hunter ordered brandy, George was driving. Annette said, 'When we were leaving, Floy said to me, "Edward is our Nemesis".'

Hunter said, 'No, he isn't, their entire bloody life is their Nemesis, it's only just caught up with them because of Daisy.' His voice was cold. 'I blame them. They protected their good name. They sacrificed Daisy. I thought they were caricatures, Ealing comedy. Floy, her sensibility, her refinement, her – selfishness. Daisy was the catalyst. Trying to protect Floy she lost her life.'

George said, 'They had a long history, how could you find your place in it.' He didn't expect an answer. 'Well, Sheldon, at least you're fed and watered.' What comfort could he give beyond that?

Good old George.

In a quiet time together, Annette said to James, 'Daisy never seemed real.'

'She was real enough, so physical, so graceful.'

'Yes, but it's as if she couldn't be held accountable for the things that happened around her because… I'll tell you what she said to me once. "When I walked through Bankhill, the perfection of the houses, the gardens, it was like a stage set, in its own hush, in its own time. The frontages just – cardboard propped up by timber – and behind their facades…nothing. No people. No real life. That's where I am." I said, no, that seemed so bleak, so nihilistic.'

'Yes, well, they are just bricks and mortar, at huge prices —' James began.

'Yes, but shut up. Your everyday, commercial, pragmatic world – it was nothing to do with her, and she knew it. She was caught in an emotional vortex, she lent herself to the lovely deceptions, the re-enactments of the Mannering existence – because it all made sense to her. Can't you see that? Oh, hell,' she fumbled for her handkerchief.

'You know what,' James said gently, after a while. 'I think you should tell Hunter that. It might help him.'

'Do you think?'

'Mmm. Try to manage it without weeping, will you?'

Hunter had woken when it was still dark and the sky full of stars, then the lonely dawn began to lighten beyond the skyline. He got up and drove to the woods where he'd walked with her. Cobwebs hung, spangled with dew; the trees blurred behind shrouds of mist; autumn had already begun to steal away the summer.

Later, her funeral was held in golden autumn light. He knew the poems and music she loved. Floy had insisted that his wishes took priority. She had friends all around her, several Mannering relatives in various stages of dignity and eccentricity. Daisy's mother remained untraceable; which somehow seemed appropriate; having cared so little for her daughter in life, how could she trespass here, amongst people who loved her.

Daisy's bewilderingly many friends meant nothing to Hunter, except Ellie, who had flown over from New York – a dark-haired girl heartbreakingly Daisy in her leggy stride, the balance of her vital body. She gave Hunter a fierce hug, whispered, 'I'm angry, too. Angry as hell.' In Clive there was no bright debonair trace; subdued, he carried out his social role impeccably, his lost looking, quietly companionable young man at his side.

At least he had his love, that's more than I have, thanks to you and Floy.

Even while his friends and colleagues were all around him; while he endured the obsequies, suffered the tide of loss for her bright, quenched being, he wondered how long he would rage against them for sacrificing Daisy.

Annette touched his arm. 'Mr Hunter, I'd like to tell you something.'

He was in a distant place, unyielding, looking only to sustain himself – no contact had relevance for him.

'Something Daisy said to me.'

They went to sit in a laurel arbour. His eyes full of questions, his strong face full of longing when anyone spoke Daisy's name, that they might have some particle of her life that had evaded him, and could now come into his possession.

Annette, managing not to cry, told him what Daisy had said to her about how important Bankhill was to her. And then, speaking on her own behalf, 'They always cared for her, valued her, her happiness meant a great deal to them. They were – generous, guv, the way she was.'

Yes, but it didn't ease the pain. Perhaps it might, in the future, on some descending scale of his grief.

His time with her so short. It began when he saw a ghost, and afterwards, so often the obliqueness in his glimpses of her. The first time he went to Fairmead, irresistibly drawn to look back as they drove away to where she stood by the white gates.

When she had come to speak to him at Talbot Way...it was their first touch, she had taken his hand. How did you grasp the glitter of a dragonfly's wings?

Seeing her from his office window as the summer storm fled and she walked away through a common landscape of grey buildings and glittering puddles. And the complete need of his life said, *wait, wait. I'm here.*

And then, the railway at Bankhill, their heedlessness, hugging each other on the bridge. And the silver tracks below, the filaments of past, present…

Darkness.

Now, yes, his ghost.

Bankhill.

Where she would always be.